"Out of the corner of her eye, she saw Dr. Reit's panic-stricken face as he leaped forward. For an instant his hand closed about her wrist. But before he could pull her free, an unearthly wind seized her. Sheila screamed as she was dragged away from Dr. Reit—

Then she was tumbling helplessly down and down into a dizzying world of stormy blue . . ."

*　　*　　*

And so begins Sheila McCarthy's incredible journey to the mysterious and magical world of Arren—a whole dimension away from home! Join her as she meets a beautiful, silver-haired Unicorn Queen, a handsome boy warrior who battles for good in an evil-torn land, a dark wizard who vows to capture Sheila, a gentle unicorn named Morning Star, and magical creatures, both good and bad, as you share . . .

THE SECRET OF THE UNICORN QUEEN
THE FINAL TEST

Will Sheila ever find her way back home?

THE
SECRET OF THE
Unicorn Queen

❧ BOOK THREE ❧

The Final Test

DORY PERLMAN

Beaver Books

A Beaver Book

Published by Arrow Books Limited
62-65 Chandos Place, London WC2N 4NW

An imprint of Century Hutchinson Ltd

London Melbourne Sydney Auckland
Johannesburg and agencies throughout the world

First published in the United States by Ballantine Books 1988
Beaver edition 1989
This edition published by arrangement with Ballantine Books,
A Division of Random House, Inc.

Copyright © 1989 by Parachute Press, Inc.

Made and printed in Great Britain
by Courier International Ltd
Tiptree, Essex

ISBN 0 09 965490 3

1

Celebration!

The clatter of hoofbeats broke the stillness of the moonlit night as the unicorns and their riders climbed the rocky mountain path. The unicorns moved with determination, their proud, single-horned foreheads bent to the task of carrying the riders to safety.

Sheila McCarthy held tight to the black mane of her creamy white unicorn, Morning Star. Her hazel eyes gleamed, and her body seemed to tingle with excitement. She was riding away from a battle that had been both terrifying and thrilling. In all the fourteen years of her life she had never felt anything like the exhilaration she felt this night.

She looked around quickly at the women warriors who surrounded her, each mounted on a strong, majestic unicorn. There was regal Nanine, gentle Pelu, rough Myno, and haughty Dian. Kara the archer rode her unicorn with Lianne, her delicate dark-haired sister, in the saddle behind her.

Ahead of them all, their leader, Illyria, the Unicorn Queen, rode strong and steady. Her long silver-blond hair glistened in the moonlight, as her pure white mount, Quiet Storm, led the rest toward a safe haven.

"Yip-yip-yaaaaahhhhhhh!" Myno cried out exultantly. Her cry was echoed by joyful shouts from the others. They had reason to feel good. They had just out-witted and outfought the emperor Dynasian and his soldiers, who had tried to trap them at his mountain fortress. Now they were riding away from near death, and they were still together—hardly injured and triumphant.

The band's only male member, Illyria's brother, sixteen-year-old Darian, rode hard to catch up with Sheila. Sailing comfortably along on the back of his ebony-black unicorn, Wildwing, he looked as though he had been born in the saddle.

"We did it!" he shouted to her, his voice full of pride.

"We sure did! We sure did!" she shouted back with a wide smile. Darian and Sheila had worked together to help defeat Dynasian. They had been the first to uncover the plot that would have doomed them all to captivity or worse. All they had gone through together had strengthened their special feelings for each other, feelings they had shared since the first day Sheila landed in this strange world.

Darian tossed back his handsome head of tousled brown hair and laughed with sheer pleasure at the memory of their victory. "You fought like a she-bear back there," he said. "I'd be glad to fight beside you any time."

"If you can catch me," she challenged, squeezing Morning Star with her knees as a signal for the unicorn to gallop even faster. She did this to hide the blush of pleasure she felt rising at Darian's praise—and because she knew he would race her and she wanted to race. She needed to vent the feeling of wild energy she felt whirling around within her.

I did fight almost as well as the others, she thought proudly as she bent low over Morning Star's neck, her long auburn hair sailing out behind her. *Who would ever have believed it? I've changed so much since leaving home.*

Leaving home. It hadn't exactly been Sheila's idea, but when she tripped over Dr. Reit's cat and fell through the transport window of his still-experimental Molecular Acceleration Transport Device, she had landed in this unfamiliar, magical land. Her only chance for survival depended on her learning to fight, hunt, and ride as well as these women warriors who had adopted her.

At first she had felt sorry for herself, but that hadn't lasted long. She soon found herself caught up in their quest to save the wild unicorns. It was a challenge that had tested her bravery to the limit, but she had come to feel as passionately committed to freeing the unicorns as did the others.

I've done it! I really belong, she told herself as she galloped on, enjoying the feel of the night breeze in her face and the power of the unicorn beneath her. Her sword slapped against her thigh and her lavender tunic flapped freely beneath the tough leather breastplate that she wore to protect herself in battle. The only thing out of place was her school backpack, which bounced hard against her back.

Darian was pulling ahead now. Sheila leaned farther forward. "Go, girl, go," she whispered to Morning Star. The unicorn whinnied and picked up her pace. In minutes, Morning Star and Wildwing were neck and neck. At home Sheila might have considered the idea of letting a handsome boy like Darian win. No more. She had learned to play to win as never before. Now she liked the new feeling of physical and mental strength she had discovered in herself. She surrendered herself fearlessly to the unicorn's lightning pace, just as Illyria had taught her.

"That's enough, you two," came the commanding tones of Myno, Illyria's second in command, as she galloped up beside them. Sheila and Darian responded to Myno instantly, slowing their unicorns to a canter.

Myno didn't seem angry, though. Her usually serious eyes twinkled with happiness. "Don't weary these unicorns; they've been through enough for one day," she said. "We all have."

"Ha, Myno, your age is showing," Darian teased. "Sheila and I feel fine."

"Quiet, you pup," Myno shot back merrily. "I can still give you a hiding if I choose." Sheila looked at the strong redhead, who had once been a slave in Campora, and didn't doubt her words for a minute. "Keep the pace," Myno told them. "We still have a climb ahead of us."

As Myno rode ahead, Darian and Sheila rejoined the other riders. The group's happy chatter died down as the twisting mountain path gave way to a sharp upward slope. Sheila groaned; the ride was getting harder. "It looks as though Illyria plans on taking us to the top of the mountain," she murmured to Darian.

"It does," Darian agreed. "I suppose she wants us as far from Dynasian's troops and Mardock's spells as we can get."

At the mention of the wizard Mardock's name, Sheila grew silent. Her joy was replaced by dread. Dynasian's wizard was as evil as he was powerful—and he had sworn to get Sheila if it took all eternity.

"What's wrong?" Darian asked, concern in his dark eyes.

"It . . . it's Mardock," Sheila admitted. "I'm in big trouble with him."

"But, Sheila, you've beaten him before, and you still have your magic bag," he said, nodding toward the knapsack on Sheila's back.

Sheila sighed. The bag contained just what she had been carrying that day after school when she stopped off at Dr. Reit's to ask for some help with her science paper—a pack of matches she had needed for a school lab experiment, some makeup, a mirror, a tape player, some tapes, some books, and a few other everyday things like that. At least they were everyday things back home. Here, a stick that could light fires was pretty special. People even thought it was magical—something that had earned her a reputation for being a student sorceress.

"Darian speaks the truth," said the elegant Nanine, riding up alongside them. Sheila noticed that the golden powder Nanine always wore on her brown skin glistened in the moonlight. This small vanity and Nanine's royal bearing were the only indications that Nanine had once been a princess. She had joined Illyria's band to escape an arranged marriage to a man she didn't love. That life must seem as far away to Nanine as Sheila's life in the twentieth century seemed to her, Sheila thought.

"Your magic is strong, Sheila," Nanine continued. "I remember when you threw one of Mardock's own spells back upon him."

"And we all saw you use your spirit box to confuse the guards when we rescued half the herd in Campora," Darian added.

That had been a Michael Jackson tape. "I keep telling you none of that was magic," Sheila said. "It was just using the stuff we all take for granted in my world."

"But it seems to me you come from a magical world," Darian insisted.

It was all so odd. In this world magic was real— real in a way she had only read about. But, Sheila realized, thinking of the space shuttle and heart transplants and all the technological wonders of home, her times were magical in their own way. Her friends here would certainly be amazed if they could see her home with its TV, VCR, dishwasher, washing machine, and microwave oven.

A wave of homesickness passed over Sheila. Maybe someday she would see home again—maybe not. Dr. Reit had come through the transport device and almost been able to take her home, but it hadn't worked out, and who knew if she would ever see the kindly old scientist again. She tried not to think of home, but when she thought of Mardock, she wished she were safe in her own bed.

"There's not enough magic in this bag to fight Mardock," she said with a weary sigh. "The next time I meet him I'm afraid I'll be out of tricks."

"I think not," said Nanine kindly. "Those are only tools you carry in your bag." Nanine reached over and tapped Sheila's breastbone with long elegant fingers. "The real magic comes from in here."

"I wish I believed her," Sheila murmured as Nanine rode away.

"Don't worry, I'll stand by you," said Darian. "We all will."

Sheila shivered and then shrugged her shoulders. "I'm not going to think about it anymore. I plan to enjoy our victory tonight."

Sheila and Darian rode on in silence as Illyria led them through a narrow, twisting passageway in the rocks. The stone floor of the tight corridor sloped up, and Sheila was glad the unicorns were so nimble-footed. The loose rocks would have tripped up a mere horse.

Suddenly the passageway widened and the unicorn warriors found themselves in the middle of a small grotto. High walls surrounded the grotto on all sides.

Illyria rode Quiet Storm into the center of the hard, grassless spot. "This is where we will rest for tonight," she announced in her full, melodic voice. "These walls will shelter us, and it is a spot known to few others. We will be safe here."

The riders began unsaddling and preparing to bed down, but Sheila stayed a moment in her saddle and watched Illyria. The young woman they called the Unicorn Queen was speaking gently to Quiet Storm as she stroked his white mane. It seemed to Sheila that at that moment this fierce and brave woman looked like the beautiful, gentle girl she must have once been. But that was before Dynasian's troops raided her father's mountain horse ranch, killing her parents and driving the unicorns her father cared for into captivity.

Only Illyria and Darian had survived the raid—and they had vowed to set the unicorns free.

Illyria's animal-sharp instincts made her sense Sheila's gaze, and she looked up quickly, meeting Sheila's eyes. She left Quiet Storm and walked toward Sheila. "You fought well today, my girl," she said warmly, her ice blue eyes shining. "I owe you much for using your head and your heart to help me."

These words from the woman Sheila had come to admire so much melted every fear and misgiving. Sheila looked at Illyria and took in the fine, delicate features so in contrast with the rough, deeply tanned skin. The silver and leather armor she wore over her patched crimson tunic was pieced together from parts found along the way, but on Illyria they looked just right, royal even. From the moment Sheila first saw Illyria, she knew she had never known anyone more imposing or confidence-inspiring. Illyria had won Sheila's complete loyalty as she had won the hearts of all her warriors.

"I'd gladly do it all again," Sheila answered.

Illyria laughed wearily. "Let us hope you will not

have to, but with half a herd left to free . . . who can tell? We will hope for the best." At that a new energy seemed to seize Illyria, and she walked briskly back to the center of the grotto.

"Hear me!" she shouted, raising her silver-braceleted arms. "Until this moment there has not been time to thank you all for fighting so valiantly. You have earned your rest, and I will gladly open a satchel of rich foods I was able to grab from the stores of Dynasian's fortress." Illyria laughed at the thought. "Tonight we feast—but no need to thank Dynasian, I'm sure he'd rather see us starve."

"Let's eat!" Darian shouted, and a happy cry went up from the group.

"The first to taste of Dynasian's luxuries will be Lianne," Illyria continued, indicating the frail girl who stood beside Kara. "We welcome her to our group with great joy."

For Kara the greatest victory of the day had been finding the sister she had long sought in Dynasian's prison. Lianne looked happy but tired, and confused by this wild group her sister was now a part of. Sheila smiled. She could understand Lianne's feelings exactly—not much more than a month ago she had felt the same.

Illyria unhitched a heavy bag from Quiet Storm's saddle and lifted it with all her strength. She dropped it with a thud and spread it on the rocky ground. Sheila's mouth watered instantly. Before her lay silvertopped jars of nuts, smoked fish wrapped in spun-gold paper, hard sausage, cheeses, fresh fruit, candies, and brightly colored, flavored waters in jade-inlaid silver flasks. Sheila knelt and lifted a gold, ruby-encrusted lid from a round box and found a cake covered with honey and almond slivers.

"This would make an attractive center for my shield," said Dian, taking the jeweled lid from Sheila. Of all the warriors, Sheila found only sixteen-year-old Dian hard to take. And the feeling was mutual. Sheila had unseated Dian as the baby of the group, and, more important, Dian resented the special relationship Sheila had with Darian. There was no love lost between the two girls.

"I saw it first," Sheila protested, not so much wanting the lid, but resentful of Dian's presumption on taking it from her. Sheila snatched the lid back from Dian and turned her back on her.

A strong hand lifted the lid out of Sheila's grasp. "Eat all you want," said Myno, "but there'll be no squabbling over the wrappings. Older and wiser heads shall decide how it is best used. Some will be melted to mend armor, and some will be traded for supplies."

"See what you've done," Dian hissed at Sheila, flipping her luxurious black hair over one shoulder, her brown eyes glancing around at the others. "I'd planned to share the jewels with you; now we get nothing."

"This is no time for bickering," said Myno, putting her hands on their shoulders. "Eat before it is all gone."

The girls joined the others in sampling the captured delicacies of Dynasian's sumptuous larder. Sheila grabbed a crisp, red apple and savored its sweetness. She knew that apples didn't grow in this part of the land. Dynasian had obviously imported much of this food. And after a rough diet that had sometimes consisted of roasted bat, Sheila enjoyed the food thoroughly.

As they ate, Myno built a fire, and Pelu pulled a small, carved flute from her frayed leather boot. Lifting it to her lips, she blew a lively tune. The petite woman's ash-blond braids shook as she played, and the tiny pieces of silver she kept tied to the ends of the plaits clinked like little musical bells. Sheila put down the hunk of honey cake she held and smiled at the group's nurse and resident veterinarian. Pelu's gentleness was like a touch of her mother's own caring ways.

Dian began to sing to the tune of Pelu's playing. Despite their problems, Sheila had to admit Dian had a beautiful voice. The others joined her in the singing, and as they did, the music picked up in tempo.

Nanine jumped to her feet and began to dance in the flickering light of Myno's fire. The exotic princess from a land far south of them moved with the ease of a river. The gold cord she had twisted around her dark forehead flashed in the firelight, and her waist-long curly black hair flew out around her as she spun faster and faster.

The others clapped along and marveled at the lion-like grace of their friend. When the dance was done, Nanine threw her head back proudly as the others applauded.

"I have an idea," said Darian. "Let's get Sheila to teach us one of her songs from home."

"Yes," Illyria agreed. "A wonderful idea."

"I don't think you want to hear me sing a solo," Sheila said with an embarrassed laugh. She knew her singing voice wasn't one of her strengths. "Still, I can give you some music."

Sheila reached over and rummaged in her pack until she found her tape player. Sheila slid a Bruce Springsteen tape into it and pushed the "play" button. Bruce belted out a hard-driving rock 'n' roll number while guitars played and a saxophone wailed in the background.

"It's too loud," said Myno gruffly.

"I like it," said Darian.

"Me, too," Dian admitted grudgingly.

Nanine started to dance again, fitting her body surprisingly well to the foreign sound of rock music. "I could like this," she said as Bruce rocked on. Soon all but Illyria and Myno rose to their feet and began moving to the music, laughing as they waved their arms and shook all over.

"You look foolish," scolded Myno, still on the ground.

"Come on, my serious friend," said Illyria, rising and pulling Myno up with her. "We are still young enough to learn new ways."

Just then a cloud seemed to block the full, round moon. Looking up, Sheila saw that it wasn't a cloud at all. Twelve huge eagles were soaring through the sky, their powerful wings silhouetted in the moonlight.

Sheila snapped off the music and looked at Illyria. The Unicorn Queen held her arms up to the sky longingly.

"Laric!" she cried in a voice filled with emotion.

2

❈❖❈

Riding Through
the Night

The eagles circled ever lower until two dozen avian feet touched the ground. Slowly their forms blurred into a shimmering golden glow. Sheila had seen this amazing transformation before, but it always made her jaw drop in wonder.

The golden light continued to grow until Sheila and the others had to shield their eyes. Then it dimmed, and in the place where the eagles had been stood twelve strong warriors in leather armor, their long capes hanging around their broad shoulders. The most startlingly handsome of them was a man with dark shoulder-length hair caught back in a rough cord. His almost-black eyes flashed with energy as he looked around quickly. When he spied the object of his search, his face opened into a wide smile, and he stepped forward, holding out two strongly muscled arms.

In an instant Illyria was enfolded in those arms. "My love, my love," she murmured as he stroked her pale hair. The pair stood entwined, Prince Laric's red and gold cape wrapped around them. Laric closed his eyes, and his commanding features softened with joy. The two lovers hadn't had a chance to speak during the battle. But Laric had been there when Illyria needed him most—just as he always seemed to be.

"Let these lovers coo," said Myno heartily to Laric's warriors. "We shook Dynasian's tree today and look what fell out of its branches." Myno pointed to the feast set out on the ground. "If anyone deserves to partake, it is you good soldiers who saved our hides from Dynasian's butchers."

"The moon is full, so we will gladly make merry while we can," replied Cam, a stocky blond-haired man with a pug nose and twinkling eyes. The other men laughed happily at his words and set to eating and joking with the women. They were all good friends by now, having battled Dynasian side by side more than once.

Sheila looked up at the full moon and then over at Laric, who was now talking quietly with Illyria in a corner of the grotto. *What a sad love story*, she thought. Through the course of their many nights spent talking around the campfire, Illyria had told her all about her romance with Prince Laric.

Laric and his men had been cursed with one of Mardock's cruel spells and had been turned into eagles. Laric was a mage himself and had tried a counter spell, but he hadn't been fast enough to completely overturn Mardock's evil. Still, thanks to his efforts,

Laric and his men were able to tranform from men to eagles at will during the five days and nights of the full moon.

Illyria had met him when she was just the simple daughter of a horse rancher. He had been beaten by Dynasian's soldiers, bespelled by Mardock, and left on the side of the road. Illyria nursed him and fell in love with him, thinking he was just a handsome stranger in need of her care.

On the day that the moon waned and Laric saw what Mardock's spell had done to him, he left suddenly, unable to say good-bye to the girl he loved. He had sensed she would stay by him no matter what, and he had not wanted to ask such a sacrifice of her. He left Quiet Storm, the beautiful creature he had called up with his magic, to look after Illyria, and he flew off to find his men, who had also fallen under Mardock's wrath.

He couldn't have known that fate would change his sweet love into the hard-riding, quick-witted Unicorn Queen. But one day he saw her again as he was soaring through the sky. She was riding with her women across a dusty plain, determined to reach faraway Campora and free the unicorns. That day he vowed to watch over her and protect her in any way he could.

Pelu had begun playing her flute again, and the men and women were dancing, holding each other loosely around the waists in a dance that called for them to step out with one leg and then spin together three times. After each series of steps Pelu picked up the tempo. The couples spun ever faster until they broke apart, breathless with laughter.

Darian came up beside Sheila. "Want to give it a try?" he asked.

"I've never done that dance, but it's a little like the polka we learned to do in gym," she answered. "I'll give it a try." Darian clasped his hands behind her waist, and she did the same. Raising their right legs and stepping, they joined the other dancers, who were whirling and laughing.

Sheila smiled at Darian as they turned, and he returned her smile. It was nice to be doing something fun with him—and it was nice having him so near. Sheila didn't want to admit it, but she realized that somewhere along the line—she couldn't say when— she had begun to think of Darian as being more than just a friend.

"Whew!" she gasped when the dance ended. "That was fun."

"Illyria and Laric shouldn't be so serious," Darian said. "I'm going to get them to join the dance."

Darian and Sheila looked over at Illyria and Laric and thought better of the idea. The two were talking intently. Sheila saw Laric shaking his head no. Illyria wore an anxious expression and seemed to be insisting on something. Again Laric shook his head no. Sheila couldn't believe it. Where they actually having a quarrel?

Laric held Illyria's wrist, but she broke loose and

walked away from him over toward the fire, where the others were, eating and dancing.

She put her hand on Pelu's shoulder to stop the music. Sheila glanced at Laric and saw that he wore an expression of exasperation as he looked at Illyria. "I'm sorry to halt the merriment," Illyria began in a serious tone. "Prince Laric has given me news that I believe is of utmost importance to my warriors."

"Illyria, it is not your concern or theirs," Laric broke in.

"Indulge me, my love," Illyria said gently. "When I lay out the situation before my warriors, they will be free to decide for themselves."

Every eye was on Illyria as she stepped closer to the fire, the flames bathing her in golden light. "As you know, Laric has been searching his books of magic for a way to break Mardock's foul spell," she addressed the group. "Now he may have found a way to do it."

A murmur of excitement rose among the men and women. "He tells me that during his time spent in the enchanted grove of the ancients, he spoke with the learned astrologers who dwell there—"

"The what?" Myno broke in, puzzled.

"The ancient women who have studied planets and who are descended from women who studied the planets before them, as did their mothers before them," explained Cam. "They watch the skies and keep records of how planets and stars move. They have records that date back almost to the beginning of time."

"It sounds like a peaceful life," observed Pelu.

"Those old crones nearly scared me to death!" cried Gebart, a young man with short black hair. "They must have been over two hundred years old. I couldn't wait to get out of that grove."

"Scared of an old woman?" Dian giggled flirtatiously.

"They had hands bonier than my eagle talons," he told her.

"These astrologers are wise," Illyria continued, "and they have told Laric that in two days hence there will be a full lunar eclipse."

"So? We are not afraid of the dark," said Kara.

"Laric has learned that Mardock's spell can be broken only during the darkness of a lunar eclipse."

"We're free!" cried a large man with a full red beard.

"It's not that easy, Atmar," Laric spoke up. "To be free of Mardock's spell we must drink a potion known only to him while the moon is dark. We must somehow find that potion now, or we won't get another chance for many years."

"And we will do everything in our power to find that potion, and to free our friends of this tyranny," Illyria said emphatically. A rumble of assenting voices swelled at Illyria's words.

"I cannot ask you to do this," Laric protested. "There is a price on your heads, and you must give all your energies to freeing the unicorns."

"Are we not friends and allies?" Myno challenged.

"And haven't you come to our aid many times?" Nanine added.

"You see?" said Illyria, whirling around to face Laric. "My warriors feel as I do. We will face this together."

"Do you all agree?" asked Laric with concern.

"We agree!" came the unified voices of the unicorn warriors. Even the unicorns whinnied, seeming to take up the cry.

"You are true friends, indeed," said Laric, putting his arm around Illyria. "I fear we must cut short this feasting if we are to accomplish this. The only place to find Mardock and uncover the spell is in Campora, which is a goodly ride from here. I am loath to take you back to that city, which is so dangerous for you. I will not blame anyone who chooses not to go."

In silent answer to Laric's last statement, the women began to reassemble their gear, while Darian stamped out the last of the fire. Within a half hour all eight of the unicorn warriors, plus Lianne, were mounted and ready to go.

Sheila suppressed a shiver of fear. She hadn't counted on returning to Campora so soon. She didn't welcome the possibility of facing Mardock again. *But how can I refuse?* she thought. *Laric has been a great friend. And it would mean he and Illyria could have a real life together. I'll think about that and not about Mardock.*

Illyria embraced Laric, holding him tightly. Then he and his men underwent their awesome golden transformation back into eagles. The unicorn warriors waved as they ascended into the night sky. "Be safe, my Laric," Sheila heard Illyria whisper.

Once the eagles were out of sight, the warriors were anxious to go. Illyria mounted Quiet Storm, who whinnied, sensing the excitement ahead. "Let's ride!" commanded Illyria in a voice that seemed to echo to the very stars in the night sky.

Instantly eight unicorns sprang forward, their hoofs beating against the ground. The far slope of the mountain shuddered, as Illyria's warriors dashed toward Campora—and whatever unknown dangers awaited them there.

Sheila gazed at the steep dirt trail that twisted down the mountain. It didn't matter how fast Morning Star ate up the distance, the path seemed to go on forever.

"If you can't go any faster, let me pass!" Dian yelled crossly as she came up behind Sheila.

Sheila was about to holler an annoyed reply when she caught a glimpse of Dian's rock-hard expression. There was something beneath that definitive self-assurance. Something vulnerable. Something scared.

She's scared to death, Sheila realized. And suddenly a flower of fear blossomed deep within Sheila as Morning Star carried her through the night, over the flat plain stretching endlessly before her. She had been on raids before. She had experienced plan-making, sneaking around guards, and all-out battles. These things had been hard and frightening, but they were nothing compared to the prospect of facing an evil wizard bent on revenge.

As Pelu's unicorn pulled up beside Sheila and Morning Star, the healer gave Sheila a gentle pat on the back. Sheila felt a spark coursing to her from Pelu's touch. She looked up and saw the large eagles soaring across the bright, round moon. She had been so busy worrying, she had almost forgotten she wasn't alone in this. She had good friends—strong, protective, and loyal friends.

"Ride to victory!" Sheila heard Nanine cry from behind her. The certainty and strength in Nanine's voice lifted Sheila's spirits.

"Ride to victory!" Sheila yelled with all her might. The shout pierced the cool night air. Sheila saw one of the eagles dip low as if acknowledging her words.

"Ride to victory!" Pelu took up the cry. Then Kara joined the shout. And Darian, and Dian, and Myno. Even Lianne, afraid and shivering behind her sister, raised her voice. "Ride to victory!" Soon the riders' voices were joined by the cries of the eagles above and the neighing of their own unicorns.

"Ride to victory!" Illyria's voice rang above them all.

Suddenly the hours of riding, the unknown struggle before them, didn't seem so overwhelming.

Filled with renewed spirit, they rode hard through the night. Sheila focused on Morning Star's shiny horn as it bobbed up and down in front of her. What a magical creature Morning Star was! She never tired, and she seemed to know which way Sheila wanted her to go without any directing. They had become so close.

Weariness began to seep into Sheila's bones as the

first pink and golden ribbons of dawn-light streaked the sky. She realized she had been up for almost twenty-four hours.

Illyria led them to the edge of the plain, which dropped off sharply all at once. The riders stopped beside her and looked into the distance at the towers that glistened in the early dawn light.

"There it is," said Darian, riding quietly up beside her.

Sheila looked at him and nodded. "Campora," she said simply.

3

The Decision

As the unicorn riders dismounted in the hills above Campora, the gigantic wings of the eagles beat through the ever-lightening sky. As if on cue, the eagle warriors touched down, and their feathered bodies began to change. Within seconds eleven of the twelve birds had transformed into strong, able-bodied soldiers. But one eagle—Sheila realized it was Laric when she saw the special black marking on his forehead—was remaining in his eagle form. His steady amber eyes seemed to study everything before him with piercing accuracy.

"What's he doing?" Dian whispered.

"He's got some magic to work," Illyria explained quietly. "He can't accomplish it in human form."

The women, the newly transformed men, and the unicorns watched with curiosity as Laric began a strange bird song. Emitting a series of low squawks, the young prince flapped his huge muscular wings. The black mark on his forehead seemed to glow.

As the performance continued, Sheila felt herself being drawn into Laric's powerful magic. She couldn't take her gaze from him. Not that she wanted to—Laric's movements were both beautiful and mesmerizing.

Suddenly Sheila was jolted out of her trance as the earth near her feet began to churn with activity. "Hey!" she shrieked.

"Ye spirits!" Dian exclaimed, her terrified face mirroring Sheila's. "What kind of demons are these?"

Then Sheila realized that it wasn't just a little plot of ground that was churning—a huge hole seemed to be opening up only inches from her feet.

"Don't worry," Illyria whispered to the frightened girls. "This is Laric's doing. The magic is working."

Suddenly a furry, round, sleepy-looking head poked its way up out of the earth. "Why . . . it's a mole!" Sheila exclaimed as the fat little creature climbed out of the newly dug tunnel. "Just an ordinary mole." The mole sniffed at Sheila a few times, then turned and ambled toward Laric.

But . . . it wasn't just *one* mole. Slowly, not far from where the first one had surfaced, moles began popping out of the ground. Ten, twenty . . . Sheila figured there were at least a hundred of them!

"By the gods!" Dian murmured, sounding stunned.

"You can say that again!" Sheila agreed.

Sheila felt a strong, reassuring hand pat her twice on the back. It was Laric—in human form. She had been so busy watching the moles, she hadn't even noticed his transformation. "Have no fear," he told her. "The moles are my friends. I used my mage's powers to summon them for help. Our little burrowing allies have dug a tunnel from here"—he pointed to the churned-up ground so near to them—"to Dynasian's palace. Dynasian's soldiers are on the alert for us. We would never be able to slip through the gates unnoticed."

Suddenly one of the moles started snuffling loudly at Laric's feet.

Laric nodded. "My little friend Mugdug says the end of the tunnel comes up right under Mardock's chamber. We'll just have to loosen some of the mortar around the stones in the floor to get inside."

"Our time is short. We must go through the tunnel and get the potion from Mardock!" Illyria said. She hefted her sword at her side for emphasis and walked bravely to the tunnel's opening. "Hmmm. Rather small," she commented as she peered into it. Then she squatted down and dangled her legs into the dark entrance. It was clear that there was no way the statuesque queen would fit through the opening.

"Uh-oh. I think we're in trouble," Sheila murmured to herself.

Illyria sighed hard, and Sheila watched her hide a dejected frown. Sheila could feel that same dejection coursing through her own body. "It looks as though the moles have failed us after all. We're going to have to find another way into the city—"

"Wait!" It was Dian, striding toward the Unicorn Queen purposefully. "Let me try the tunnel, Illyria. I'm smaller than you are. Maybe I can fit." Not waiting for an answer, Dian got to her knees and lowered herself in. "Ungg," she groaned as the sides of the tunnel pinched her ribs. Still, slowly, she was sinking out of sight. With a few more grunts and groans, she disappeared. "Pretty tight," Dian cried from below, "but I think I can do it!"

Dian could be such a pain most of the time, Sheila thought, but she had to admit that the other girl definitely came through in a crisis. Dian was willing to go through discomfort and danger—all alone—with barely a thought.

A frown crossed Illyria's face. "I can't let you go, Dian," she said thoughtfully. "I cannot send you on such a perilous mission all alone. Mardock may well be waiting at the other end of the tunnel."

Dian pushed up out of the tunnel. "I'm a warrior-woman," she said. "I have to try, even if it means risking death!" Dian spoke bravely, but no one could ignore the quaver of fear in her voice.

"No," Illyria insisted. "It is too dangerous. We will find another way."

Sheila watched, her mind racing. Whoever went down that tunnel would be walking right into Mardock's domain, practically giving herself into the miserable old magician's hands. Dian was willing to do it and do it alone. And yet, Sheila knew that if Dian could fit through the tunnel, so could she. Maybe Illyria would agree to let them go if they went together.

But . . . did she have the courage to volunteer? Mardock had vowed to get her and have his revenge in the most painful way. Should she tempt fate?

Sheila squeezed her hands together hard, the nails of one cutting into the other nervously. "I'll go, too!" she shouted. "Together we'll have a chance."

Illyria turned and a smile lit her strong, serious face. "You grow braver by the day, little one," she said, studying Sheila's face. "It's too much. We need a more experienced warrior."

"We fight as well as anyone else, why should this be any different?" Dian pressed. "We owe Laric and his men much."

Illyria sighed. "You are right. The two of you have proved yourselves many times over. Still, I do this with great misgiving. You are both so dear to me ... all right, you are the ones best-suited to this, and you are brave and capable. Go, but I beg of you, do nothing rash. Look around for the potion and get out." Sheila stared at Dian, her partner in this all-important mission. The two of them had feuded in the past, and though they had learned to tolerate each other, they definitely weren't friends. Not by a long shot. Now they would be depending on each other for their very lives! Dian was staring back at Sheila with a strange mixture of anger and relief on her face. *I feel just the way you do, Dian,* Sheila thought to herself. *I'm glad to have help on this crazy job, but why does it have to be you?*

Still, neither girl said a word. The situation was much too serious for useless bickering.

"I guess I can't take this with me," Sheila said, slipping off her knapsack. "Dian and I will barely fit through the tunnel *without* extra baggage." Trying to seem confident and careless, she dropped the bag to the ground.

"Oh, but Sheila, won't you need to take any of

your magic objects from it?" Pelu asked quickly. "In case you run into Mardock, I mean." Gracefully she bent down, picked up the knapsack, and handed it to Sheila. "I'm sure you can fit some small thing in your— *pocket.*"

Pelu spoke the last word in English. Pockets didn't exist in this world. Instead, people carried small, essential items in pouches that hung around their necks. When Sheila had shown Pelu the pockets in her jeans, the other warrior had been astonished—and pleased, too, at such a wonderful idea.

Sheila took the knapsack from Pelu. Her friends believed she could take something special and powerful from that bag—something that would help her fight Mardock's magic. Only she knew the truth—she didn't really have any magic at all. Sheila stared forlornly at the tunnel and thought about going off empty-handed to face her worst enemy.

Well, Sheila thought, *some of the stuff in the backpack has helped me in the past—like the pocket mirror.* Quickly Sheila rummaged through the pack, looking for a little portable "magic." Working fast, she pulled out a spare pair of gym socks and a pencil case. She rummaged some more—makeup, a felt-tip pen. She decided to take the mirror. As she threw down her Spanish notebook, a small square of cardboard bearing Mookie Wilson's face came flying out from between the pages.

Sheila snatched it up. "My lucky baseball card!" she exclaimed. It had been so long since she had thought about it, she had completely forgotten that it was there. Finding it now was a miracle. *This is a good omen,* thought Sheila.

Sheila stuffed the baseball card, the little mirror, and her few remaining matches into the back pocket of her cutoffs. Then she forced a grin to her lips. If she *acted* unafraid, maybe she would *feel* that way for real. "I'm ready to go," she said seriously.

As the sky continued to lighten with the rising sun, Illyria stepped toward Sheila. "We're all very proud of you, Sheila," she said softly. "Good luck." Then she wrapped Sheila in a heartwarming hug. Sheila could practically feel the warrior queen's strength seeping into her, making her tingle with an extra bit of bravery and courage.

"We have faith in you," Laric said. "And what's more, I have something for you to take with you." Seemingly out of nowhere, the eagle prince produced a small golden disk. "This may look small and unimportant, but it holds some very strong magic."

The disk felt warm and comforting in her hand. "How do I use it?" she asked. "What do I do to make it work?"

Laric smiled faintly. "Nothing! It will know what to do by itself. It will be very useful in finding the potion. Let it lead you to the spot where you must search."

"Thanks," she said simply as she shoved it deeply into her pocket, next to the baseball card and the mirror.

As Sheila stepped to the tunnel's entrance, Morning Star hurried forward. Gently the unicorn nuzzled the back of Sheila's neck. *I love you, too, Star,* Sheila thought. *And I'll see you again. I'll get out of this alive. I promise.*

Slowly she and Dian embraced each of the other unicorn warriors—Kara, Myno, Pelu, Nanine, and Lianne. Last of all, she came to Darian. She felt such a jumble of feelings saying good-bye to him. He looked into her eyes, then pulled her close and hugged her tight. "Be careful," he whispered. Sheila nodded as he released her.

Finally it was time to go. Sheila stepped toward the passageway's entrance. Her phony smile was gone. "Okay, Dian. It's up to you and me now," she said softly.

"Yes," Dian answered without the slightest hint of her usual bravado. Dian scrambled back into the tunnel, and Sheila followed.

As Sheila dropped into the dank hole in the ground, darkness closed over her head and she felt herself sinking, sinking, sinking, toward an unknown adventure, an unknown danger.

The only thing she could be sure of was her own fear. . . .

4

❧ ❖ ❧

In Mardock's
Chamber

"Ooof," Sheila grunted as she hit the bottom of the
tunnel with a thud. The hilt of her sword jabbed painfully into her ribs. She could feel damp earth against
her bare legs.

She felt along the dirt wall of the pitch-black tunnel. "This place *is* pretty narrow. It looks as though
we're going to have to crawl all the way to Campora."

"Too bad Mugdug's friends couldn't make it any
wider!" Dian agreed, laughing nervously.

"Well, here goes nothing," Sheila said as she got
to her knees. Then, ignoring the wet muck beneath
their legs, she and Dian began crawling toward Dynasian's palace.

The trip would have taken about five minutes on
Morning Star's back, fifteen minutes if Sheila had been
running, and a half hour at a fast walk. On hands and
knees, crawling through the darkness, it took over an
hour. Sheila found that her sword kept jamming into
the side of the tunnel and then she would have to
waste time unsticking it. Worse than that, there were
places where the tunnel wasn't even wide enough to

squeeze through, and they had to claw at the earth walls with their nails or use their daggers to dig.

By the time they reached the end of the passage, the girls' knees had been rubbed raw and were beginning to swell painfully. They were covered in mud, sweat, and some unknown oozy stuff that seemed to seep out of the earth at every opportunity. They were both completely and utterly miserable. And the mission hadn't really even started yet.

Yuck, Sheila thought, wiping off her formerly lavender tunic. Her efforts succeeded only in making the mess worse. *This shirt'll never be the same again.*

Above her, Sheila realized, was the stone floor of Mardock's chamber.

"Now we've got to get into that room," Dian said, "if we can *see* well enough to do it."

"I can help with that," Sheila said. She pushed her hand into her pocket and pulled out the mostly empty book of matches. In the oozing darkness of the tunnel, she wished she hadn't wasted so many of them to amaze her new friends with her "magic power."

As the match flared, the tunnel brightened a little. "Look!" Sheila pointed. Above their heads they could see a few stone blocks, cemented in place.

"That mole was right when she told Laric the mortar was old and crumbly. That's lucky for us," Dian commented. She reached up and picked at it. A few bits came tumbling down.

"Ouch!" Sheila exclaimed as the match burned down to her fingers. She let it fall to the ground, and the tunnel was once again cloaked in darkness.

"What's the matter?" Dian asked nervously. "Why did you make the light go out?"

"It's kind of a short-lived magic," Sheila tried to explain. "I guess we're going to have to make it without light."

"Wait . . ." Sheila could hear Dian rummaging around in the dark. "Ah, here it is—a candle. It was in with the food from Dynasian's larder. I was saving it to remember last night by.

Sheila lit the elegant, spiraled candle, and once it was burning, she pulled her dagger from her hip and started poking at the cement with its tip. She hated to do it—it was going to blunt the knife terribly, and that wouldn't be good if they ran into Mardock. Still, she did have her sword.

Chipping away at the mortar was tedious work, and suddenly Sheila had all the time in the world to remember the dangers that lay before them. If Mardock was actually in the room when they got inside, they were sunk. The dungeon would be their fate, that along with slavery or . . . even execution.

Don't think of that! Sheila ordered herself. She had to concentrate on something else. It was a tactic Illyria had taught her. Fill your mind with some rote, routine thoughts, and you wouldn't have time to be scared silly. *The formulas from my algebra class back home*, she decided. Those would certainly keep her mind occupied.

Let's see. I know Ms. Klineberg was always talking about the quadratic formula in class, she told herself as she worked the knife into a crack in the mortar. *X equals . . . what?* Sheila hadn't a clue.

Well, I guess it doesn't really matter, she decided. *I mean, it's not the most useful thing for a warrior-woman to know.* Still, she felt more than a little sad as she remembered that her father had helped her memorize the formula early in the school year. What was he doing right this moment? Sitting around the dinner table with Mom? Figuring out a new computer program at work? Thinking of her?

It was too depressing to imagine it, so she went back to algebra. But the other formulas were just as foggy as the quadratic had been. After two months here Algebra II seemed to have evaporated almost completely from her brain. *Oh, heck,* she decided. *The multiplication tables are much easier, and they won't remind me of Dad. One times one is one, two times one . . .*

By the time she had gotten to nine times nine, the floor stone was loosening. At twelve times twelve it was free!

"Ooooofh," Sheila gasped as the weight of the huge rock sank onto her outstretched arms. It seemed impossible, but she had to hold the stone up, or she and Dian would be squashed. "Dian, help!" she whispered.

Dian helped her ease the stone out. "Gggughhh," she groaned as it fell with a dull thud. A trickle of early morning sunlight shone thinly into the muddy tunnel.

"Uh-oh," Sheila whispered almost inaudibly. "This is the moment of truth. If Mardock's in there, we'd better be ready to crawl out of here, and fast. Otherwise, he'll turn us into cockroaches or something."

The girls waited for a moment. There was no sound from the room above; it was empty.

"Come on!" Dian said. "Let's go." But suddenly she stopped. "What's that smell?" Along with the sunlight an evil smell was seeping down into the tunnel. "Mardock must be cooking up something strange."

"Don't think about it," Sheila whispered. "All we need is the formula for the potion that'll save Laric and the others. The rest of Mardock's junk is his own business."

Sheila blew out the candle. Then she reached up, grabbing the stones around the hole, and pulled herself through the opening. Dian was right behind her.

"By the gods!" Dian exclaimed. The place was huge: a gigantic, cavernous mess.

Piles of crumbling old books and pieces of loose parchment paper were scattered everywhere. Dried herbs hung from every available inch of ceiling space. Along one wall a long shelf held hundreds of bottles of dull-colored liquids and powders. Clearly they were the very stuff of spells, the nasty potions Mardock used to bring misery to his unfortunate victims. None of the bottles were marked, so obviously Mardock knew their varied contents by heart.

"I hope I never get the chance to find out what's in those bottles," Sheila murmured with a shiver.

Filth caked the floor, and Sheila was hardly surprised when a rat scurried past her and Dian. Disgusted, she turned away. She wasn't afraid of the rat . . . there were things much more sinister to fear.

As if to prove she wasn't afraid, Dian walked straight to a large urn and pulled off the top. As she did, something came springing out of it. "Aaag!" Dian shrieked as the thing popped into her face.

It was a two-legged toad—its missing legs had obviously been chopped off for some evil purpose or another. Then half a slug crept out of the pot. The slug was followed by a bat with only one wing. Dian looked shaken, and though she continued looking around the chamber, she was subdued and very cautious.

Sheila began searching the top of a long table. She opened a small gray box. Some unknown gray powder, with a foul odor, lay in the bottom. *Could this be the potion?* she wondered.

Out of the corner of her eye Sheila caught sight of a bolt of shimmering golden cloth that was draped over a small stool near the tunnel. *Strange,* Sheila thought. The cloth's glimmering beauty seemed so out of place in the dirty, dank room. She was about to reach down to touch it when she remembered something Pelu had told her: Magicians often used such beautiful items in their wizardry. The cloth must be enchanted.

Sheila cringed to think what horrible effect the enchantment of Mardock might have on whoever received this cloth as a "gift." She moved away from the golden bolt and continued looking around.

Soon she noticed the huge hearth in the far corner of the room. Red-hot coals burned against the stones and a gigantic iron pot sat directly on top of them. The contents bubbled madly. *That pot,* Sheila thought, *is the source of the stink in here.* Suddenly something slithered to the top of the pot. *Something alive,* Sheila realized with sickening amazement. It looked like an octopus's arm. Sheila wanted to gag.

Pushing back the desire to vomit—and a very strong urge to run away as fast as she could—Sheila turned away from the pot. She had to find the formula. But how? In the disorder of the cluttered room, the thing she sought could be anywhere. In one of those dozens of bottles. Or written down as a recipe hidden at the bottom of one of the many piles of papers. Or— Sheila shuddered at the thought—even stewing in that pot of living soup!

As Sheila watched Dian open yet another bottle and sniff it, a horrible thought swept into her mind. If they kept messing around with those magic potions, they might end up accidentally bespelling themselves, just by spilling some of the horrid stuff on their skin.

As Sheila stood there, bewildered, she began to feel something warm in the right back pocket of her cutoffs. "The magic talisman!" she exclaimed. "With everything we've been through so far, I completely forgot about it. Laric said it would lead us to the potion."

Sheila pulled out the disk and held it in her palm. As she watched, the trinket glowed white, then gradually faded to dull silver. Laric had said the disk would know what to do. Now was the time to test it.

Slowly, nervously, Sheila stepped toward the shelf of potions. The disk glowed a faint gold. But as she continued walking toward it, the disk immediately cooled off again. She moved back in the opposite direction, and it increased in brightness.

It was like a game of hot and cold. The disk shined brightly when she came closer to the potion and turned dull when she moved away from it.

"I hope this doesn't take too long," Dian said as the glowing gold directed Sheila around the room. "The more time we spend here, the more likely we are to run into Mardock."

Sheila didn't answer. The disk, she realized with distaste, was leading her ever closer to the awful pot of live octopus. If *that* was the formula, she was in trouble. The thought of filling a bottle from the huge kettle made her sick. But the disk was glowing yellow, then orange, then a full gold as she stepped toward the pot. The octopus arm thrashed within it like some kind of enchanted sea monster. Barely daring to look, Sheila thrust the disk toward the pot. It faded to a colorless gray.

"Thank goodness!" Sheila murmured. But . . . where *was* the formula? There were no bottles of powder, no piles of writings here. Had the disk led her on a wild-goose chase? Had it wasted all that precious time for *nothing*?

Suddenly the disk felt heavy. Sheila tried to let go of it, but it seemed stuck to her hand. Slowly, involuntarily, she was being drawn to the floor.

"Unhhh," she gasped as she hit the stone. The disk went spinning out of her hand, suddenly and inexplicably released from its gluelike hold. It skittered across the floor, and Sheila chased it. She couldn't afford to lose that disk. Not now. Not when she was so close to finding the formula.

But the disk was glowing brightly. It was impossible to lose track of. "Look!" Dian exclaimed. The disk had come to rest on a single sheet of yellowed parchment. "That's got to be the formula for the potion!" Dian gasped excitedly.

Sheila agreed. Curiously she picked up both the parchment and the disk. The paper was covered with odd, slanting writing.

"What does it say?" Dian burst out.

Sheila shook her head slowly as she perused the strange writing. "I can't understand a word of it. Still, from the way the disk was glowing, this has to be it."

"Maybe it's in some sort of code," Dian said.

Sheila nodded. "Could be. And I bet Laric will know how to decipher it."

"Now that we've got what we're looking for," Dian urged, "we've got to leave. We've already been here too long."

"You're right. Let's get out of here," Sheila agreed. She turned toward the hole in the floor. But as she did, a faint sound made her stop in her tracks. A key was rattling in the ancient, rusted lock of the door to the room.

Sheila's heart sank. Somebody was coming . . . and there was only one person who was likely to have the key to *this* godforsaken place.

Their luck had just run out. Mardock had arrived.

5

❧❖❧

Death Sentence

The entryway to the tunnel was fifty yards away from them, across the room, and it would be just seconds before Mardock appeared. In a flash, instinct took over, and the two girls were moving. Pumped by adrenalin, their legs sped them toward the hole in the floor—and safety.

Ahead of her Sheila watched Dian slide into the tunnel. A few instants later she was doing the same. The sound of the door scraping against the floor filled the room. Sheila and Dian had made it. Except . . .

Except for the gaping mouth of the tunnel. Mardock couldn't help but spot it. And if they tried to escape through the passageway, he would follow and they would lead him right to Illyria and the others! They had to hide the hole. But how? They had just seconds to act.

Suddenly Sheila felt her hand growing warm. Laric's disk! She had been so scared, she had forgotten all about it. And now it was heating up again, practically burning in her fingers. Clearly the powerful magic piece was giving her the message that it could help her out once again.

Sheila opened her hand, staring at the talisman. Without warning the disk flew from her hand, sailing toward the hole in the floor. "What are you doing!" Dian gasped angrily. "Why did you throw that thing away? We've got to get out of here!"

"It wasn't me!" Sheila shot back. She was too shocked to explain what had happened.

Meanwhile, the piece of gold flew back into the room and, guided by its own extraordinary power, slammed hard into the enchanted bolt of cloth that sat near the tunnel's opening. The material floated to the ground. Magically, it fell across the hole, hiding it to perfection. And as the cloth settled, Sheila heard voices—two of them—as footsteps sounded in the chamber above.

"Good work," Dian whispered shakily. "Hiding the tunnel will give us a little more time to escape." Sheila knew that Dian had turned and started the long crawl back out of Campora, expecting Sheila to follow.

But Sheila didn't follow. "Wait!" Sheila whispered. "Laric's disk. We can't just leave it. What if Mardock finds it?"

"No!" Dian whispered the word, but her tone was fierce. "That disk is not worth dying for, and—"

Dian broke off as a few words from above stopped the two girls dead. "We'll kill those unicorns once and for all, and be rid of them." Mardock's sharp voice pierced their hearts like a dagger.

Sheila grabbed Dian's arm and squeezed tight. For a moment the horror of what had been said stunned her. Already the land suffered because the unicorns were in captivity. How much worse would it be if they were destroyed! Sheila glanced at Dian. "Now we've *got* to stay—"

"Agreed!" Dian whispered, her tone completely changed now. "I'll risk my life for the unicorns. We've got to find out everything we can and bring the information back to Illyria!"

In the dark the two girls waited, shuddering with fear, for the next words from above. "Kill the unicorns . . . yesss," a second voice hissed like a snake slithering. "It's a wonderful idea."

Sheila knew immediately who had uttered the terrible words. That cold, pitiless voice could belong to only one person. Dynasian! And no one but the evil emperor could agree to such a cruel and stupid plan.

"Let me tell you a bit more," Mardock said, false humility covering his contempt for the emperor. As Dynasian's most trusted adviser, he flattered the emperor at every turn. Yet the sorcerer was a master of manipulation.

"As you know, your most defiant subjects have made the unicorns a rallying point," Mardock explained. "They've been building a revolutionary organization around the idea of freeing them. Dispense with the miserable animals, and you'll break the rebellion, plain and simple."

Another flash of fury rose into Sheila's throat. Anger was replacing fear.

"That was my idea exactly," Dynasian purred.

Sheila could picture him stroking his pudgy, overfed face as he thought. "We'll murder the beasts in a public display—right in the central square of Campora—so that everyone can see." He chuckled. "The rebels will look on, hopeless. And *I* will be victorious!"

"Very good," Mardock sniveled obediently. "You've come up with the perfect plan. But, My Leader, I have a small suggestion. Those unicorns have magic power. It would be a shame to lose it all when they die." The sorcerer hurried on, not giving Dynasian a chance to realize he was being manipulated. "You see, I think you can kill them and get their power for yourself. I'll check my spell book and tell you how it's done."

Down below, in the dark, soggy tunnel, Sheila sucked in her breath. So *that's* what Mardock was after. The unicorns' magic! Above, she could hear him flipping through the pages of one of his huge magic books.

"How much do you want to bet he knows exactly what that spell is," Sheila whispered to Dian. "That rummaging through the book is just to please Dynasian. Mardock had the whole thing planned all along."

The rummaging stopped. "Ah, yes, here it is," Mardock said greedily. "All we have to do is cut off the horns and grind them into powder. A tiny pinch of it on my tongue, and I'll increase my powers at least ten-fold."

Ten-fold! Sheila didn't dare believe it. Mardock was barely beatable now, as he was. If he got any stronger, the forces of good would never be able to gain the upper hand—and she, herself, would be completely doomed. Mardock would be able to kill anyone just by *thinking* about it.

"Wait a minute," Dynasian was saying. "A pinch on *your* tongue? What about *my* tongue. They're *my* unicorns. *I* want the power!"

Dynasian sounded like a spoiled three-year-old throwing a tantrum—a very *dangerous* three-year-old.

"*Of course*, on *your* tongue, too, My Leader," Mardock hastened to add. "We'll keep it, just for the two of us."

But the wheels were turning in Dynasian's conniving mind. "I've got an even better plan. We'll give it away."

"*What?!*" Even a practiced politician like Mardock couldn't keep the shock and desperation out of his voice. "The powder would be a thousand times more precious than gold. You *can't* let it go."

Down below, Sheila imagined Mardock's expression. The sorcerer was watching his longed-for powers slipping quickly out of his grasp, before he even had a chance to taste the unicorn powder. He must look like a cross between a wounded water rat and a rattlesnake ready to strike. But then again she herself was pretty confused by Dynasian's bizarre turnabout.

"Oh, don't worry, you fool," Dynasian replied airily.

Only Dynasian was stupid enough—and powerful enough—to call Mardock a fool.

"We won't *really* give it away," Dynasian explained. "But we can *pretend* to do it. We'll promise the stuff to the ten subjects *I* judge to be most faithful. Everyone will be trying to impress me in order to get the powder. They'll stuff the palace with expensive gifts. They'll be tripping over their own sandals to please me.''

Greedy old creep, Sheila thought.

Mardock was having no trouble agreeing—once he realized that he would still get his magic powder. ''Genius, sheer genius,'' he wheezed. ''People will betray their own grandparents if they seem disloyal, just to be in better favor. You'll crush the revolution—''

''And get richer—'' Dynasian added.

''All at the same time. There won't be a rebel left in the entire country!''

That's what you think! Sheila felt like shouting. She knew for a fact that there were plenty of rebels who would never give up, who could not be bought at any price, and who were not very likely to be caught by any of Dynasian's mealy-mouthed subjects.

''And I know the perfect time to stage the execution and 'reward' your loyal subjects,'' Mardock continued. ''I've done some calculations with my star charts. Tomorrow night there will be an eclipse of the moon. The darkness at the moment when the moon is blotted out would provide a wonderful cover for replacing the real unicorn horn with a substitute powder.''

''Then it's settled,'' Dynasian's voice cut through. ''We'll publicize the event today. Then, tomorrow night, we'll slaughter the unicorns and grind their horns in public. When the moon goes black, we'll substitute talc for the magic powder!" He laughed, delighted at the treachery of his plan.

"As I said before, you're a genius," Mardock praised him.

Dian tugged at Sheila's tunic. "All right. We've got the information we need. Let's go!"

"No!" Sheila whispered back. "We still have to get Laric's disk. If Mardock finds it, who knows what he'll do with it. It's very powerful—and besides, it might tip him off to Laric's plan."

"What are you planning to do? Go up and ask Mardock to return the disk?" Dian was getting angry.

"Mardock will eventually leave, and then we can go up and get it," Sheila answered.

"We have to tell Illyria about the plan to kill the unicorns. We can't afford to get caught now," said Dian. "Come on, Sheila. Remember what happened when you went back to pay the cloth merchant after we took the fabric in Ansar that time? You barely made it out of there alive."

"Dian," Sheila said. "I'm staying. I have to get the disk. You go if that's what you think is best."

"Fine!" Dian snapped. "You obviously haven't learned a thing about doing what you've been instructed to do. You always have to do everything your own way."

"You do things your way, I'll do them mine, okay, Dian?" Sheila angrily turned away from Dian. She wanted to get out of there as much as Dian did, but she couldn't let Mardock get that disk. There was no telling what havoc he would cause if he possessed its magic.

When Sheila turned back to Dian, she saw the girl was already crawling away from her down the tunnel. "Wait, Dian, the potion," Sheila whispered as loudly as she dared. It was no use. Dian was swallowed up into the darkness of the tunnel almost instantly. In her anger and eagerness to leave, Dian had forgotten to take the parchment that had the potion written on it.

Sheila told herself it didn't matter. She'd soon be crawling out of the tunnel right behind Dian, and she would hand the parchment and the disk to Laric herself. She pictured herself doing that, and she felt warmed by the image of a smiling Laric and Illyria thanking her for a job well done.

In another moment the comforting mental image was gone as she focused her attention on the sounds in the chamber above her. From the muffled tone of their voices, it seemed to Sheila that Dynasian and Mardock had moved away from the tunnel's entrance. In another minute she heard the unmistakable creak of a door opening and closing.

Sheila waited a moment, listening. Was it only Dynasian who had gone, or had Mardock left with him? The moment lengthened, but all she could hear was the key turning in the lock. No extra footsteps. Not a sound at all. She had gotten her lucky break. The room was empty.

Sheila raised her arm, ready to sweep away the

golden cloth that covered the tunnel. She stopped herself abruptly. She had forgotten—it might be dangerous to touch the fabric.

She slipped her dagger out of its sheath and, using the tip, inched the cloth away from the hole. Light from inside the room spilled into the tunnel, making Sheila blink. When she opened her eyes, she realized the terrible mistake she had made.

The chamber wasn't empty. Looking up, Sheila stared directly into Mardock's fiendish black eyes.

6

❧❖❧

Trapped!

"Y-you?" the cruel sorcerer sputtered. An expression of stunned amazement etched across his twisted features.

Sheila dropped her dagger, fell to her knees, and started crawling into the tunnel as fast as she could.

"No, you don't!" Mardock's voice boomed. "You're not getting away from me *this* time!" In an instant Sheila felt a shock of energy hit her. She was being dragged back through the tunnel, and there was nothing she could do to counter the strength of Mardock's magic. When she reached the tunnel opening, Mardock grabbed her, his thin strong hands wrapping painfully around her forearms. As he jerked her up to face him, he pulled her sword from its sheath and threw it toward the bubbling pot on the hearth. The tentacled arm reached up and pulled it down into the bubbling brew. Mardock shook Sheila fiercely. She couldn't escape. Sensing that struggling would only encourage Mardock to squeeze harder, Sheila stopped fighting.

Pressing through her own terror, Sheila opened her

mouth to speak. "H-how d-did you kn-know I was down in th-the tunnel?" she stammered. She knew she hadn't made a single unnecessary sound as she had waited below.

Mardock laughed. "Magic!" he replied.

Still, Sheila's careful eyes took in a pair of scissors and a spool of golden thread lying near the glimmering, magical cloth on the floor. Suddenly she knew exactly what had happened. Mardock hadn't known she was there at all! He had simply been getting ready to turn that cloth into a beautiful, lethal garment at the exact moment that Sheila had pushed it aside with her dagger. It had all been a matter of very bad luck!

"Now, tell me, my dear"—Mardock bared his yellow teeth, like a dog getting ready to attack—"what *were* you doing in that tunnel beneath my room? Trying to steal a little magic?"

Sheila just stared at him. There was no reason to give Mardock a single shred of extra information.

"So you won't answer? Well, no matter. I'll *force* the truth out of you." Mardock dug his long nails into her arm and seemed to be contemplating some gruesome torture. Sheila didn't want to give him more time to think.

Summoning up every bit of strength within her, Sheila struggled against Mardock's ever-tightening grip. "Unngh," she groaned. Mardock laughed.

Desperate, Sheila chomped down on Mardock's hand. "Aaaagh!" The startled wizard pulled away. Here was her moment! She ripped herself away from the horrible sorcerer. Falling to her knees, she made a desperate grab for the magic disk. She could feel her fingers graze its shining surface . . .

The tip of Mardock's boot got there just a second faster. Lightly he kicked it just out of Sheila's reach.

"So that little piece of gold is what you were after, is it?" Mardock nodded with his sharp little chin toward Laric's disk. "Well, let's find out what's so special about it." Grinning triumphantly, he leaned down. Feeling utterly lost, Sheila watched him scoop it up.

Mardock screeched in pain. Cursing, he dropped the disk. A gaping wound stretched across the palm of his hand, and a faint burning scent reached Sheila's nose.

"Miserable forces of Light!" he spat. On the floor at his feet Laric's disk lay in a melted lump. It still glowed, however, with powerful light.

Suddenly Sheila remembered something Pelu had told her long ago. When the forces of Light met the forces of Darkness, nature seemed to go haywire. When Mardock had picked up the disk, his own evil forces had collided with Laric's good ones. Neither his hand nor the piece of gold could stand the contact.

"You little snake!" Mardock growled at Sheila, rubbing his hand in pain. "How dare you try to destroy me!" he raged. "Well, your plan has failed. You'll pay for this—this and all the other trouble you've caused me." The hatred in his voice was so violent it made Sheila wince.

Despite her fear of Mardock, Sheila was alert enough to notice something strange. The disk was inching its way across the floor. *It's trying to help me!*

she realized. *It's buying me one last chance to escape. And I've got to be ready when the moment comes.* She thought of the magical formula stuffed in her pocket. *Laric and his men are counting on me, too.*

"Yes, you've got me!" Sheila agreed. She had to divert Mardock's attention, keep his gaze away from the disk until it could achieve whatever strange thing it was attempting. "I'm your prisoner, and I see now that there's no escape."

Mardock ceased raging and looked at her coolly. "I'm glad you've realized that. It will make things easier on *both* of us."

Sheila stole a covert glance at the disk. It was sliding quietly toward the pot of bubbling octopus on the hearth. *What's it up to?* she wondered.

She didn't have to wait long to find out. Suddenly the disk flew toward the living stew. An octopus's tentacle reached out of the caldron to grab it and . . .

Ppppppppppppppowwwwwwwww! Forces of Light met forces of Darkness. The pot, the octopus, and the hearth exploded in a blinding flash of fire and light.

Sheila didn't wait to see Mardock's reaction. The instant she saw the cauldron blow, she scrambled toward the entry to the tunnel. She dived through it, mud splattering around her.

Sheila guessed no one in history had ever crawled as fast as she did at that very moment. And she was sure no one had ever hoped so hard.

"Stop right there!"

Sheila's hope disintegrated as Mardock's furious

voice reached her ears. A fizzle of sickly green energy crackled all around her. Suddenly the tunnel ahead of Sheila crumbled into nothingness. Her heart felt like crumbling along with it. She was caught again, trapped. And this time Laric's disk wasn't going to be there to help her out. This time there would be no escape.

Still, she had her dagger!

She pulled the sheathed dagger from her belt and shoved it into her pocket along with the formula and her lucky baseball card. The handle stuck out above the fabric, but she quickly hid that by tucking her tunic down over it. It bulged, but it wasn't *too* noticeable if you didn't look too hard. Maybe, just *maybe*, she would get through a search and still hold onto the things she needed most.

"Get out of there!" Mardock demanded. "Before I have to do something *really* nasty."

"Oooooookay," Sheila murmured under her breath. It would be better not to enrage Mardock further. Feeling thoroughly miserable, she crawled once again to the mouth of the tunnel and pulled herself out to face her doom.

"I've had enough of your trouble!" Mardock shouted. "And I am going to end your wretched life— believe me!" He lifted his hand cruelly. The stench of evil, green energy seeped out of it. Slowly Mardock pointed one finger at Sheila. He intended to kill her right there and then, that was clear.

Sheila bit her lip. She refused to show her fear. If

she was going to die, she would die bravely. Just when she thought it was over, a sickening smile spread over Mardock's face, and he dropped his hand.

"Yes, I'll end your life. But *not* here and not now. I've got a better idea. I'll give you to my liege, Dynasian. And tomorrow night he'll slaughter *you* along with the unicorns!"

Mardock swept toward the door, his ebony robes swirling behind him like a storm brewing.

"Guard!" he called into the corridor outside.

A soldier in royal armor appeared, one hand at his sword's hilt. "Yes, Revered Sorcerer!" he cried obediently.

"Get this girl out of here," Mardock commanded. He pointed rudely into Sheila's face. "Take her to the prison! And . . . don't bother to be gentle about it!"

Sheila pressed her lips together hard as the leering soldier stepped toward her. *They won't see me acting afraid*, she thought with determination.

Still, when the guard roughly grabbed Sheila's arm, she couldn't help but let a tear escape from the corner of her eyes. It wasn't just herself she was crying for. The formula for Laric's men was in her pocket. If she was lost, the formula would be lost with her, and the men would remain bespelled by Mardock's power forever.

She should have given Dian the formula. She wondered if Dian had escaped—or been caught in the tunnel collapse caused by Mardock wizardry.

She bit her lip hard to stop the tears. *Please be all right, Dian*, she prayed, trying not to think of the girl crushed under all that dirt. *Be all right—and bring help!*

7

❦✦❧

The Secret Potion

Sheila lay on dirt-caked straw in a tiny prison cell, trying not to notice the two skinny rats who were eyeing her hungrily. A weak trickle of sunlight filtered into the filthy room through a single window, secured by sturdy iron bars. In the far corner of the cell a human skull sat atop a pile of bones. Its death's head grin seemed to mock Sheila. *You'll never get out of here*, it said, laughing. *Just like me.*

Sheila had never felt so alone. "I will not cry," she murmured with determination. "A warrior-woman has to be brave. . . ."

But suddenly she remembered something Illyria had told her long ago, when she had just been starting her warrior training. *Being brave isn't about never feeling scared—it's about doing the right thing in spite of being scared.*

And all at once the tears came. Great, big, salt-laden tears. They poured out of Sheila's hazel-green eyes, soaking her unhappy cheeks and the filthy straw beneath her.

As she lay sobbing, her mind began an unhappy

tour of everyone she had ever known and loved in her short life. They paraded before her eyes, a sad procession of lost friendships. There was her best friend from home, Cookie, and sweet old Dr. Reit. An image of Illyria's rugged yet gentle face, along with Darian and Morning Star and Myno, floated before her. At this point Sheila even missed Dian.

And as she remembered everyone she knew, the sobs kept coming. The woman warrior had transformed back into a frightened, helpless fourteen-year-old. Sheila couldn't imagine ever not feeling scared again.

Half an hour later Sheila's tears had almost dried. *There is only so long you can keep up this kind of misery,* Sheila decided. Finally she just felt empty and hollow. The most painful pangs were gone, leaving just a dull, aching throb in the center of her chest.

Pushing herself off of the grimy straw bed, Sheila leaned against the cold stone wall, letting the faint ray of sunlight warm her face. She had been in this prison once before. Illyria had been with her then, and the place hadn't seemed nearly as lonely or tedious. Now she had only the rats for company.

Still, even the well-trained Unicorn Queen hadn't been able to slip through the bars of the tiny window or pick away at the hard mortar that held the huge wall stones in place. They had used a trick to get out that time. Luckily, Dr. Reit had appeared in the nick of time and scared the guard so badly that Sheila and Illyria had been able to escape. *Oh, if only Dr. Reit were here now*, Sheila thought. But he wasn't, and Sheila had no possibility of escaping. She would just have to fill the time and wait ... for her execution.

Shoving her hand into her pocket, she pulled out everything she had hidden there. First came her dagger, then the matches. Her hand mirror had cracked during all the rough treatment the guard had given her. Last were her lucky baseball card and the paper with the formula for Laric's men on it.

Idly she picked up the knife and began cleaning underneath her fingernails. The weapon was useless now—it wouldn't help her get out of this place. Still, it was somehow comforting to have it around. She was glad the guard had missed her few possessions when he had searched her. No one in Campora *had* pockets, so the guard hadn't looked for Sheila's.

Sheila groaned in frustration. She grabbed the baseball card from the floor and glared at it. What good would knowing Mookie Wilson's batting average do her now? She shoved the useless card back into her pocket. Then Sheila picked up the formula for the secret potion. It was written in complete gibberish— probably some kind of code. Well, maybe she could figure out what that code was. It wasn't likely she would ever pass such information on to Laric, but it would fill the time.

Heaving a sigh, she studied the strange words. SOUZS GDSZZ: AWL NOBUO BIHG, GDFWBU KOHSF, OBR VCBSM. At the bottom of the page was the tiny notation—$A = 25 \times \frac{3}{5}$.

It was only one line, but it held the key to a magical mystery that kept twelve good people enchanted. And . . . Sheila had the feeling she could crack it. Dr. Reit had taught her a thing or two about using logic to break through seemingly impossible problems. It was all part of the scientific process, he had told her. Well, all through her adventures in this distant land she had been using "science"—the inventions of modern-day life crammed in a jumble in her backpack—to overcome Mardock's magic. Why not try again?

Sheila settled back against the bumpy stone prison wall. Smoothing the paper she had stolen from Mardock's chamber, she trained her eyes on the mysterious words once again.

There was always a logic system behind a code, Dr. Reit had said. According to the scientist, codes worked on one of two very simple principles. The first was to substitute one word for another. If you wanted to say *diamonds*, you use an innocent word like *apples* or *potatoes* or *bubble gum*.

The second kind of code involved substituting one *letter* for another. You might substitute X for B or L for X. Then you would get gibberish. Obviously, that was the method Mardock had chosen. Now all Sheila had to do was figure out which letters to exchange.

Well, the paper itself seemed to hold a clue. "$A = 25 \times \frac{3}{5}$." That had to be the key. Mardock must have written it down to remind himself of how to crack this particular code—he probably used dozens of different ones for all his spells.

But . . . somehow the strange equation reminded

Sheila of something. Something distant, from a far-away life. Something from . . . her algebra class!

"Hmmm," Sheila murmured thoughtfully. "If this were an algebra equation, the first thing I'd do is simplify the whole thing. Let's see . . . twenty-five times three is seventy-five. Divide all that by five and you have fifteen. . . ."

So . . . A equaled fifteen. But how could a letter be a number? Maybe the fifteen stood for something else. Like . . . like maybe the fifteenth letter of the alphabet. Quickly Sheila counted forward. The fifteenth letter was O. And if the letter A was written as O, then maybe B was set down as the letter *following* O. That would be P. And C would be the next letter after that—Q.

Quickly Sheila cleared a place in the straw. The floor was so dirty underneath it that she could scratch letters into the filth. She retrieved her dagger and, using its tip as a pen, scribbled down the twenty-six letters of the alphabet. Then underneath she wrote a *second* alphabet, but this one started with the letter O.

Let's see, Sheila thought. The first word was SOUZS. Using her decoder she translated. S would equal E. And OUZS would be AGLE. The first word was EAGLE! That was it. She had cracked the code—only six more words to go.

It didn't take Sheila more than five minutes to unravel the rest of the message. It read: EAGLE SPELL. MIX ZANGA NUTS, SPRING WATER, AND HONEY. Simple!

And yet, it wasn't really simple at all. Sheila had never heard of a zanga nut. It was probably one of the many exotic luxuries Dynasian had imported into his palace from faraway lands. Sheila's heart sank . . . even with the formula, Prince Laric couldn't hope to get enough zanga nuts to make twelve portions of the potion, certainly not by tomorrow night.

Suddenly Sheila noticed a faint drumming sound seeping into her cell from the street outside the prison. Sheila tried to ignore the sound as she searched her mind for some way—any way at all—to get a few dozen zanga nuts in one day. But the sound wouldn't go away. It kept worming into her head like a lawn mower that had been left on.

A *lawn mower?* But there weren't *any* motors in Campora. . . .

Dropping the slip of paper with the decoded message, Sheila jumped to her feet and ran to the window. The opening was too high. Still, if she used all her arm strength, she could probably hoist herself onto the stone window sill.

The motor sound throbbed insistently outside. Inside, Sheila slowly managed to hoist herself onto the skinny ledge. She stared outside, taking in the ground about six feet below her.

"Dr. Reit!" Sheila shrieked. It was unbelievable, but there he was!

The scientist's shaggy white hair was flying in three different directions, as usual. His grease-stained lab coat hung on his thin frame like a sack, and he was very happily and securely putting along on a shiny red moped!

"Dr. Reit!" Sheila called again.

"Sheila!" the scientist exclaimed. He smiled up at the window and waved.

As he let go of the moped's handlebars, it tipped dangerously. His face twisted into a comical grimace, and he made a mad grab for the bike, righting it just before it tumbled him onto the stone pavement.

"Oh, dear," he murmured. Then he returned his attention to Sheila. "Thank goodness, I've found you. I was afraid the Molecular Acceleration Transport Device's tracking device was on the blink."

"Dr. Reit, *what* are you doing on that moped?" Sheila's voice cracked with laughter. The scientist was hardly the motorbike type.

Dr. Reit grinned. "You'll recall, speed is the key to the Molecular Acceleration Transport Device. The faster I go, the longer I can stay—and the more likely I am to be able to rescue you." But as he looked at Sheila through the bars of her prison cell, his expression turned somber. "But I can hardly save you if you're locked up in prison, can I?"

"No, Dr. Reit, you can't!" Freedom was so near and yet so thoroughly impossible. The thought brought back Sheila's tears—tears she had thought she had sobbed out of her system. But she couldn't let them out. Even *with* the moped Dr. Reit's visit to Campora would probably be all too short. He could begin fading out at any moment, sucked back home by the machine he had invented. They had a lot of information to exchange before that happened. There was no time for crying.

"I wish I could show up in your cell," Dr. Reit was saying. "Then I could get you out of prison and Campora, all in one stroke. But I don't think I can do it. The Molecular Acceleration Transport Device just isn't that precise about where it sets me down. . . ."

"Look, we don't have time for that right now," Sheila broke in. "Everything's going wrong. The unicorns are going to be slaughtered, Laric's men are about to miss their only chance to break the spell, and . . . and I . . ." But Sheila stopped herself from telling Dr. Reit about the awful death sentence that hung over her own head. There was nothing he could do to help her.

Still, maybe Dr. Reit *could* help—not to set *her* free, but to save Laric and the others.

"So here's what I want you to do," she said quickly. "Find Laric's band and tell them the potion is made out of zanga nuts, spring water, and honey!"

"Hmmm, zanga nuts, eh? That's a new one," he said. Sheila knew his brilliant mind was already at work on the formula.

"And what about you, Sheila?" Dr. Reit asked, his deep, dark eyes brimming with concern. "Are you safe where you are—at least for the moment? At least until I can come back for you?"

Sheila paused for one, frantic moment. Should she tell him the truth? If she didn't, she doomed herself—Dynasian was going to kill her tomorrow night. Dr.

Reit couldn't save her—he had already told her that. . . . No, she couldn't tell him.

"Don't worry, I'll be fine," she said softly. "Tell Illyria not to worry about me. With the unicorns about to be sacrificed, there's just too much for her to do to help me."

Dr. Reit stared at her sadly from the ground below, his long lanky legs balancing him precariously on the moped. "Sheila, I can't do what you're asking," he said. "There's no way for me to find Laric. The Molecular Acceleration Transport Device's tracking device isn't set to this frequency. You're the only person in this world whom I can trace—and even *that* is pretty difficult."

As she listened to his words, a twinge of desperation twisted up inside Sheila's stomach.

"Don't give up hope," Dr. Reit said.

He was beginning to fade, his form flickering in and out between Campora and his lab back home. In a few minutes, Sheila knew, he would be safely back home, far from the land of unicorns, cruel dictators, and magic.

"I'm sure Illyria and Laric haven't given up on you. I bet they're looking for you all over Campora. They'll find you in time, and you can tell them everything they need to know about the potion."

Sheila let out a long, miserable sigh. "Thanks, Dr. Reit," she said, even though she didn't have much faith in what he was saying. "Maybe things *will* work out for Laric." *And for me*, she thought desperately.

"I'm sure he'll get his potion in time," Dr. Reit

nodded, though his head was barely more than a shadow at this point. "Actually, that's an interesting formula you mentioned. Zanga nuts, spring water, and honey. Odd but . . . it sounds rather familiar, somehow." It was just a murmur of his voice that whispered the final words. With one more weak flicker he was gone. His last word echoed back through the many dimensions of time: "somehow . . . somehow . . . somehow . . ."

Sheila stared down at the spot on the ground where Dr. Reit had been. Then she pressed her lips together, willing herself not to cry, and slid off the window ledge.

She was all alone now, alone with two crucial pieces of information. And there was no way to get them outside her musty prison. No way whatsoever.

8

Laric's Sacrifice

A rough scratching sound was rousing Sheila from her sleep. "Five more minutes," she mumbled, thinking for a moment that she was home and her mother was waking her for school.

Sheila hadn't slept for more than a day, and so despite her terror at being imprisoned in this squalid cell, she had been unable to keep her eyes open a moment longer and had fallen into the deep, dreamless sleep of total exhaustion.

The noise persisted, and slowly it dragged Sheila into consciousness. Rubbing her eyes she remembered, dejectedly, where she was. A patch of white moonlight that shone through the window onto the floor was the only illumination in the otherwise pitch-black cell.

Clink, clink, crunch. Where was that noise coming from? She followed the sound to the window. It sounded as if someone was scratching at the window sill with a knife.

Pulling herself up to the window, she came face to face with Laric and Cam, who were chipping away at the stonework around the bars of her window. "I hope

I'm not still asleep and dreaming," she whispered happily.

"We're real, don't worry," Laric said with a quick smile.

"How did you get into the city without being spotted?"

"Flew, of course," Cam answered with a wink.

"That's right, I almost forgot," Sheila said. She noticed that their daggers sparkled and flashed lightly as they worked. "You almost have that bar loose," she observed, new hope surging back into her.

"These daggers hold magic of their own," Laric told her, not stopping his work for a second. "They are made of hammered diamonds, a gift to me from the swordsmiths of the Far East."

Sheila pulled her dagger from her pocket and joined the effort. One bar started to wobble. Red-faced with effort, Cam and Laric grunted as they pulled the bar from its stone casing.

"Hop down and lay this gently on the floor," Laric instructed Sheila. "We don't want any clanking bars alerting the guards."

Sheila did as she was told and then climbed back to help them work on the second bar. "Did . . . Dian make it back?" Sheila asked.

"Muddy and bruised, but in one piece," Cam said, wiping the sweat from his brow. "It was close, though; the tunnel collapsed not ten feet behind her just as she climbed out."

Sheila heaved a sigh of relief. "One, two, three, pull," Laric told Cam as they heaved the second bar from the window. Again Sheila climbed down and placed it quietly on the floor.

"One more and I bet I could squeeze through," Sheila said, climbing back up to the sill. Laric and Cam's hands flew with almost lightning speed. Sheila almost thought she saw sparks flying as they worked. "Listen," she said, "I guess Dian told you that the disk led us to the potion. I figured it out. It's zanga nuts, spring water, and honey."

Laric and Cam exchanged glances. "Zanga nuts, eh," said Laric unhappily. "I don't know where you'd find a zanga nut in this part of the world."

"I've seen them south of here in Kumuru," said Cam. "A strong flyer might be able to make it in time, if he never rested."

"I am not so sure," Laric disagreed, as he pushed the third bar off its base with all the strength in his body. With the bottom free, he and Cam set to work chipping away at the top of the bar.

Sheila could almost taste freedom. "What is a zanga nut anyway?" she asked.

"It's a nut that grows in very warm climates and is—" Cam started to answer her, but suddenly broke off. A sound had alerted him to danger. "What was that?" he whispered to Laric.

Sheila turned with a start at the sound of a key grating in the lock of the huge iron door of her cell. "Hop down and pretend to be asleep," Laric instructed, "and pray they don't notice these loose bars."

Sheila watched for a second as Laric and Cam transformed themselves into eagles. The guards entered the room more quickly than she had expected. She was just dropping from the ledge when they found her.

One guard grabbed her roughly by the arm. "Climbing out the window!" he shouted, mistakenly thinking she was heading up instead of down. He looked up and saw the missing bar.

"How did you do that?" he shouted, shaking her roughly.

"I've heard this one is a sorceress," said the second guard.

"I'm taking you to Mardock now," said the first guard, pushing Sheila toward the cell door.

Just then a sharp *caw* was heard overhead. Laric swooped into the room and dived for the first guard. In bird form he had been able to squeeze through the gap in the bars. Behind him Cam also attacked the guards, his wings flapping furiously around their heads.

"I told you she was a sorceress!" cried the second guard. He whipped out his crossbow and took aim, but Laric was too quick for him. Before the arrow left the bow, one powerful wing knocked the bow from the guard's hands, and the other wing swatted him to the floor.

Two more guards charged into the cell. Cam and Laric were busy with the first two guards. Instinctively Sheila snatched her small dagger. With one heedless dash she came up fast on a third guard, who aimed a steel-tipped arrow at Laric as he flew overhead. Her dagger caught him in the shoulder.

"Aaaaaaahhh!" he shrieked, dropping his bow and clutching his arm.

Sheila staggered back, stunned by her own actions. As she stood staring at the bloody gash she had inflicted on the guard, a sword descended toward her from behind.

"Broaaaaaaaaa," Laric screamed, swooping toward the attacking guard. He lifted him from behind, his talons sunk into the guard's thick shirt. He picked the guard up and dropped him with a thud to the ground, knocking him unconscious.

Cam had sent the remaining two guards fleeing for help. The coast looked clear for them to make their escape. The two eagle warriors settled on the sill and pecked frantically at the third bar they had almost loosened. Sheila scrambled up quickly to join them.

Crnnnnnnng, the third bar fell to the floor.

"Brooaaaak!" Cam cried triumphantly. He squeezed through the window and hovered in the air just outside. Sheila scrunched through behind him and edged herself out to the corner of the sill to make room for Laric. She was summoning the courage to jump down the six feet to the ground when she heard a strangled shriek of pain behind her.

Turning, she saw Laric plummet to the ground. More guards had rushed into the cell and one had fired at him, piercing his wing.

"Laric!" Sheila shouted, freezing in place. His injured body lay perfectly still . . . as still as a corpse.

"Rfffffaaak!" Cam cried. He flew over her and one

sharp talon caught her tunic. With amazing strength, he flipped her onto his back and instantly took flight.

"No!" Sheila cried uselessly as Cam flew higher into the sky. They couldn't leave Laric behind!

An arrow whistled past her ears. Then another. But Cam was too fast. He lifted into the night, and not one of the barbs found its mark.

Sheila held on tight. The image of the eagle prince's deathly still form burned in Sheila's mind. She buried her face in Cam's downy soft neck and let the tears pour down her cheeks.

9

❧ ❖ ❧

Preparing

Lianne bent the bow back, pulling with all her strength. *Thwang!* The arrow sailed through the bright morning sunlight toward the painted straw target a hundred yards away . . . and fell twenty feet short.

A small moan escaped from Lianne's throat. "Ohhhhh," she groaned. "I'll never be able to do this."

"Don't worry," said Sheila. "It can be frustrating at first. Believe me, I know."

When Sheila had arrived at their warrior camp on Cam's back early that morning, the other unicorn riders had already been hard at work. Illyria had barely given her a chance to rest after her ordeal in the jail before assigning her chores to do—which meant honing her archery skills, as well as helping Kara prepare Lianne for the upcoming battle that evening.

Kara turned away from the fallen arrow and, stepping up to her sister, gave her a gentle hug. "Don't feel bad about missing the target," she said patiently. "It takes practice, Lianne. This is only your first lesson. Of course you're no expert yet."

Lianne frowned. "But this band is a team. If we're

going to free those unicorns tonight, everyone has to shoot well!''

A look of despair passed over Lianne's tender features.

Watching her, Sheila recognized that mixture of dejection and hopelessness. After all, it hadn't been long ago that *she* had been the one learning to shoot. She knew how it felt when the lesson wasn't going well, when your arms ached from hours of target practice, and it seemed as if you would never get it right.

''It's hard to concentrate today—for all of us,'' Kara said. She dropped her bow onto the grassy ground and sank down on the green beside it, sighing.

''We don't even know if Laric is alive,'' Sheila said, dropping down beside her.

''I hate Dynasian and his horrible city,'' Lianne said emphatically.

Sheila understood exactly how Lianne felt. She gazed out across the grassy, wooded hills spread before her. Just beyond them and out of sight was Campora. Campora, where the unicorns waited patiently to be rescued.

Where was Laric—dead or alive?

A few flashes of brightly colored tunics caught Sheila's eye as the warriors wove in and out of the trees, doing chores and caring for their own battle-ready unicorns. Their fatigue didn't seem to slow them down in the least. They just kept working at whatever needed attention, preparing for the hard operation ahead of them.

Further down the hillside, beside a small brook and beneath a sun-bleached weeping willow tree, Illyria sat alone, bent over her work. Thick strands of hair had escaped from the mass of plaits coiled on top of her head. They hung like trails of a silver vine over her shoulder. Holding a rock in one hand and her sword in the other, she drew the flat edge of the blade repeatedly over the stone. The Unicorn Queen was sharpening her weapon.

Sheila turned back to Lianne. "If you think it's hard for us, think about Illyria. She's in love with Laric."

Lianne's eyes widened. "I've noticed. Yet she doesn't even seem sad or afraid. It's . . . it's almost as if she doesn't really care about him."

Kara shook her head. "Of course she does! She feels the loss, deeper than any of us. Still, she knows her grief won't serve Laric. There's too much to do before tonight. She shows her love by preparing to fight for it."

Under the shade of another tree Cam and some of the men discussed the feasibility of going in search of zanga nuts. "Laric was our strongest flier," Sheila heard Cam say. "He was the only one who could have flown to the south, found the zangas, and brought them back in time."

Lianne heard them, too. "Then all hope is lost," she said.

Sheila paused for a moment, studying Lianne. The other girl was voicing Sheila's own fears.

Sheila sighed. Despite all of her warrior training she had no encouraging words for Lianne.

Kara laid a hand on Sheila's shoulder. "Let me explain this." Looking at Lianne, Kara continued. "If we *don't* do our best tonight Dynasian wins everything. If the unicorns are killed, the plagues and famine that follow will kill thousands of innocent people. The land will be utterly blighted. Losing Laric is a sad and terrible thing. Losing the unicorns is *disaster*."

There was a moment of silence, broken by the twittering small birds as they flew through the blue sky above. How blissfully unaware of the unicorn riders' dilemma they were, Sheila thought.

Lianne pushed herself to her feet, grabbing her bow. "Well, I'll try," she said, "but I doubt I'll hit anything."

Sheila stood, too. "Maybe a little demonstration will help you get the hang of shooting." She took the bow from Lianne's hands, then held it out toward Kara. "Let a master archer show you how it's done."

But Kara shook her head and didn't take the bow. "No. *You're* the one who should show her, Sheila. After all, you couldn't even bend a bow when you first found us. Let Lianne see what can be accomplished with practice."

Sheila smiled. She knew Kara was paying her a tremendous compliment.

Sheila turned to Lianne. "The thing Kara taught me was to pretend that you are aiming at someone or something you're really angry at. It's amazing how much it makes you want to hit the target."

"So, show us how it's done. Let one fly for me—right at the guard who shot Prince Laric!" Lianne said.

"If only it were that easy to get revenge . . ." Sheila said. Projecting the image of the guard on the target, she drew the bow and fired. The arrow sailed through the air, straight and true—*thunk!* The tip sank into the straw of the target just a few millimeters beneath the bull's-eye.

"Great!" cried Darian, who had come over to join them. Sheila smiled at him.

"Beautiful shot, Sheila!" Kara seconded. "If we all fire that well tonight, we won't have a thing to worry about! Victory is as good as in the quiver."

"That *did* feel good," Sheila agreed, "but there's someone else I want to take a shot at."

She reached down and picked another arrow from Kara's lot. As she fit it into the bow, she could feel the certainty and self-assurance pouring into her arms.

Raising the bow, she cried, "This one's for Mardock!" The sorcerer's simpering smile flashed through her mind. Of all the evil characters who kept the land enslaved, he was the worst because he *knew* what would happen when the unicorns were killed. Besides, it had been *his* idea to murder them in the first place. Pulling the bow string back just a bit more, Sheila let the arrow fly.

Even before the arrow reached the mark, Sheila knew she had hit the bull's-eye dead in its center— *thunk!* The arrow sank deep into the target. Not even Kara could have hit it more truly.

"Amazing!" Lianne shouted. "And to think you were no better than I am just a month ago!"

Despite the feat she had just accomplished, despite the good feelings, Sheila knew there was another sensation pulsing through her, too. Something was bothering her, whispering madly like a frightened mouse in the back of her brain. True, she had shot the imaginary Mardock unerringly, but could she hit the *real* sorcerer when the time came?

"Illyria asked me to tell everyone that we meet in two hours to discuss her plan," Darian said, rising from the grass. "She says to rest as best you can until then."

Kara and Lianne took their leave and strolled off arm in arm.

"I'm glad you're safe," Darian said softly when they were left alone. "I wanted to join Cam and Laric, but the plan called for them to fly in, so . . ."

"Thanks," Sheila said. "I know you would have come if it had been possible."

Without speaking further Darian and Sheila began to amble toward a thick patch of trees. Behind them the eagle warriors argued over how to save Laric and find the all-important zanga nuts. The unicorn riders, too pent-up to rest, continued to prepare to infiltrate the crowd that would throng into Campora that night. Pelu sewed disguises. Nanine drew copies of a map of Campora. Myno fed the unicorns, talking to them soothingly. And the Unicorn Queen continued pounding the edge of her sword, making sure it would cut clean and quick.

"Sheila, we don't know how it will go tonight," Darian said, suddenly turning to her. "I want you to know . . . to know . . ."

Sheila waited for him to finish, gazing up into his handsome face. "Know what?" she asked gently.

"To know this . . ." he said, stepping close and kissing her lips. Their eyes met, and they kissed again.

10

❊❖❊

Festival of Darkness

The sun sank low in the sky, bathing everything in gentle golden light. Sheila watched four small redwinged birds dip and swirl as they headed toward their nests for the night. *There will be no rest for me tonight,* Sheila told herself, thinking of all that lay before her in the royal city of Campora on this fateful night.

She stood on the hillside outside Campora dressed in a scratchy gray tunic that fell well below her knees. Earlier that day, outside the gates of the city, Illyria had bartered away some of the valuable jars and boxes that had contained Dynasian's luxurious foods in exchange for the clothing all of them now wore.

These plain, dull garments made them look like typical peasants of the area.

Illyria came up behind Sheila. It seemed to Sheila that she had never looked more beautiful despite the faded black cloak she wore over her armor. Maybe it was the look of calm determination on her face—it illuminated her with an almost mystical quality.

Sheila and Illyria didn't speak. They watched silently as the plain outside Campora began to swell with people traveling to Dynasian's "celebration." They looked like flecks of many-colored confetti against the dry green-brown ground.

"Why are they even going?" Sheila asked at last, unable to bear the thought that Dynasian really did have followers who had allegiance to his rotten empire.

Illyria laughed mirthlessly. "The way the public notices were worded didn't give them much choice," she said. "The emperor Dynasian demands that his subjects appear for a celebration of their loyalty to him. Any not attending will be considered disloyal and will suffer the standard punishments for treason along with all the members of their family."

"They'd be imprisoned?" Sheila asked.

"Dynasian would think that an act of mercy," Illyria scoffed. "No, treason is punished by being slowly lowered feet first into a vat of boiling oil."

The horror of that image turned Sheila ashen, and she gulped hard. "Now I can, uh, see why they're making an effort to show up for the main event here."

"Exactly," Illyria said, putting her hand on Sheila's shoulder. "Sheila, this quest has not been of your choosing, indeed, not even of your world, yet you have served it courageously." Illyria met Sheila's eyes and smiled into them warmly.

"It hasn't been boring, that's for sure," Sheila answered lightly.

"Here is what I've been thinking," Illyria continued. "I pray we are victorious tonight, but we must all face the fact that we may not return. For us, it will mean a warrior's proud death in a noble cause. And though we love our lives, we have long been prepared to lose them fighting for this cause. And I . . . I would give my life gladly if there was even a chance that Laric is alive and I can free him."

Sheila looked at Illyria solemnly. She wasn't sure what Illyria was trying to say.

"But for you it is different," Illyria said. "There is a great possibility that your Dr. Reit will be able to take you home someday. I believe you should stay behind tonight, to save yourself for the future that is your birthright and your destiny."

Sheila let Illyria's words sink in. She was giving her permission to stay out of it. Sheila might never have to risk seeing Mardock or Dynasian again. Eventually Dr. Reit would figure out how to get her home. He would come for her, and everything would be fine—that is, if she lived long enough for that to happen.

For a moment it sounded good, but Sheila knew it was all wrong. "I can't do that," she told Illyria steadily. "I wouldn't feel right."

"There would be no shame," Illyria replied.

"For me there would be," said Sheila. "The way I got here was pretty weird, but in many ways it was the best thing that's ever happened to me. If I'd never come here, I might never have felt what it's like to depend on myself and friends for survival. I might not ever have realized I had it in me to fight or stand up to an enemy. I've found a part of me that I like a lot—

a part that's new. I've come this far; I'm not going to go backward now."

Illyria squeezed Sheila's shoulder. "I have come to think of you as a sister," she said gently.

"That makes me proud," Sheila answered with a lump in her throat. The two stood there for a moment enjoying the warmth of their deep friendship and love for each other. Sheila tried to feel Illyria's calm resolve as if it were her own.

"So be it, then," Illyria said briskly. "We will go and fight together. Let us prepare."

Sheila knew the plan. One by one they would enter the city, each doing his or her best to get past the guards at the gate without appearing suspicious. Sheila and Illyria walked back to where the others were assembled, joking nervously in their rough peasant disguises.

"It is time," Illyria announced. "We will leave in height order, so that those with the longest and quickest strides will not leave slower ones behind. In this way we will all arrive in Campora close to the same time."

"Why can't we ride?" asked Dian.

"It would be too obvious. Darian will herd our unicorns in at the last minute, saying they are a tribute from King Martna from the north."

Sheila was the smallest, so she was chosen to leave first. "At the count of one hundred the next will leave, and then the next," Illyria told them. Sheila flipped the gray hood of her tunic up over her head and took a deep breath. She walked to Morning Star and caressed the unicorn's black mane. Quickly she looked around and smiled at them all. Even Dian nodded her head assuringly at Sheila.

Darian's eyes held hers for a moment. She remembered their kiss, and she smiled. He smiled back, then she turned away and headed down the hill toward Campora.

As she got closer, Sheila became part of the crowd that was flocking in from the outlying areas from every direction. The closer she got to the gates of the city, the thicker the crowd became.

She was jostled along, soon pressed between a poor peasant woman carrying two live chickens and a rich merchant wearing a silk cape and clutching a pouch stuffed with gold coins. Both the chickens and the coins were presents for Dynasian, Sheila guessed. And they were only two gifts out of thousands that Dynasian's citizens were bringing to their leader on the night of the unicorn slaughter.

The full orb of the moon glimmered down from a star-drenched sky. In a few hours that moon would be eclipsed. By then the unicorns might be dead and their horns ground into a fine powder.

Sheila raised her eyes and saw the iron gates of the city before her, tall, ornate, and forbidding. Nervously she pulled the billowing tunic closer to her body. It itched, but it did make a good disguise, since it covered her armor and the humped form of her knapsack on her back. Sheila could feel Kara's extra bow and a quiver of arrows hanging at her side. She hoped the guards wouldn't spot it.

Ahead of her, a nasty-looking guard was talking to the woman with the chickens. She saw the guard take one of the chickens himself, and then motion the woman through the gates. So that was the story; the guards were taking bribes.

"You, girl!" One of the guards poked at Sheila's shoulder as she neared him. 'What are you bringing to the emperor Dynasian?"

Of all the questions he might have asked, this was one she hadn't planned a ready answer for. She hoped she was bringing Dynasian to his ruin, but she could hardly tell that to the guard. And if she didn't think of something fast, she'd be in big trouble.

"Ummm . . ." she stalled. Suddenly an idea popped into Sheila's head—her lucky baseball card! It was odd enough to spark the guard's interest, but not so odd that he would get suspicious.

Quickly she slid her hand under her tunic, careful not to reveal her bow. Breathing deeply, she took the card out of her pocket and flashed it past the guard. Mookie Wilson's face smiled serenely on the card.

"What's this?" the guard gasped as he took the slightly bent card from her.

"*That* is a picture of King Mookie the Met—he's very famous over in the land of Baseball." Sheila tried to sound imperious and convincing. She knew the guard didn't understand what she was talking about—and she was counting on that to confuse him enough to let her through. "Don't tell me you've never heard of him!"

"Uh, King Mookie?" The guard hesitated. "Of

course I have heard of him. In fact, he came through here last year. We were the guards who protected him." The guard studied the card closely. "What fine court artists he must have to make such a lifelike painting."

There were no cameras in this world. A photo would seem like a miracle here, Sheila realized. She screwed up her face into a condescending sneer. "The painters of the land of Baseball are known for their brilliant talents. Only a fool wouldn't know that! Why—"

"I was just testing you," the guard broke in peevishly. He clutched the photo a little more tightly. Then he motioned her to go in with the other hand.

Sheila looked at the guard. Obviously he planned to keep the card. Sheila was surprised to find that the thought of going on without it really hurt. She sighed. Well, it didn't really matter. Getting into the city and saving Laric and the unicorns did.

Sheila stepped through the huge iron gates and into the dirty, crowded streets of Campora. Sheila was amazed at the sight and size of the crowd. There were mothers with crying babies, aristocrats reclining in pillow-stuffed litters carried by sweating slaves, beggars, and pickpockets. Anxious for the action to begin, Sheila rushed to the central square.

She found it was already jammed with people. They were packed into the cobblestone area, squeezed onto balconies, and balanced precariously on the rooftops. A huge platform with stairs leading up to it had been erected in the center of the square. Sheila assumed it was from there that Dynasian planned to address the crowd.

Sheila scanned the crowd for soldiers. Their sharpened spears looked more than a little lethal. A group of them were packed tightly, close to a high pen on the far side of the platform, which was constructed of wood.

Inside the pen were the remaining unicorns. There were almost fifty of them of many sizes and colors. It broke Sheila's heart to see them pawing at the ground, their eyes wild with fear.

As she looked through the slats of the pen, Sheila saw something else that made her heart stop—a large wooden cage with an eagle in it. Laric! An ugly wound marred one of his wings and a trickle of blood wet his feathers. His wings were tied with a tight rope. And yet Sheila felt like shouting with joy. Laric was alive! The warriors still had a chance of saving him.

Sheila glanced around and caught sight of the other warriors, who were beginning to station themselves in strategic spots around the square. She saw Illyria in the crowd standing straight and tall. She suppressed the urge to wave and shout the good news about Laric. She couldn't afford to attract that much attention with Dynasian's guards on the alert everywhere.

Sheila had time to reach the spot Illyria had assigned to her before Dynasian made his grand entrance. She positioned herself just to the right of the pen as Dynasian was carried in on a litter draped with garlands of finely crafted solid-gold olive leaves.

Four little girls walked alongside the litter, carrying torches to illuminate the overstuffed emperor. A dozen slaves lifted the bed high. Dynasian lifted his fat hand in a lazy wave. His oiled hair was arranged in curls around his low forehead, and he was swathed in a billowing robe spun of pure gold that wafted around him in the gentle night breeze.

That cloth! Sheila had seen it before. Dynasian's robes were made of the beautiful golden material she had seen in Mardock's chamber. *Is Mardock's magic working for or against Dynasian?* Sheila wondered.

Behind Dynasian, Sheila spotted Mardock. Wrapped in his inky robes, he was like a puddle of night in the midst of all the torchlight. His dark form seemed to suck the light around him into the black void of his soul.

As Dynasian hoisted his massive body out of the litter and onto the platform, the soldiers roared, "Hail Dynasian! Hail Dynasian!"

The crowd picked up the chant as the guards stared at them menacingly, but Sheila could tell it lacked the conviction of true adulation. Sheila exchanged an anguished look with Kara, who stood on the steps of an ornate white building a few yards away.

Up on the platform Dynasian began his speech. "Citizensss!" he cried, hissing hideously as he spread his arms wide. "You've come here tonight to see a great event—you've come to honor me, your emperor."

Polite applause rippled through the crowd. Up

above, a single eagle whirled across the full moon. Then another, until finally nine golden eagles circled overhead. Laric's men had arrived.

Sheila saw Mardock look up nervously at the eagles. She clutched her bow, ready to shoot if he even twitched in their direction. She was afraid he would use his power against them, but hoped that he didn't want to ruin the spectacle of the unicorn's slaughter. For now he just stood behind Dynasian on the platform and glanced discreetly at the eagles overhead.

Meanwhile, the emperor continued his vile, self-congratulating speech. "I know the love you feel for me, your leader, and of course, I wish to reward you for it. The ten subjects I've deemed to be the most loyal will be gifted with magical powder ground down from these unicorn horns."

The eagles were circling nearer, closing in on the packed public square. And with each millimeter of their descent, Mardock became more and more agitated.

"The unicorns will die before your very eyes in a few moments," continued Dynasian, unaware of the threat above him. "Once the beasts are dead, my sorcerer Mardock will grind the horns into magic powder. This will be the greatest spectacle Campora has ever witnessed."

Another cry swept through the crowd, but now it was mixed with cries of horror and fear. As Dynasian paused to let his words sink in, Mardock stepped toward him and whispered something, pointing at the eagles, who were winding ever closer.

Dynasian seemed visibly shaken, Sheila thought, as she watched him confer with Mardock. The crowd began murmuring restlessly. People began pointing to the sky. Realizing he had to regain control of the crowd quickly, Dynasian signaled for trumpets to be blown from the ends of the platform. As the crowd quieted, Dynasian continued his speech.

"Perhaps some of you have noticed the birds flying overhead." Dynasian's voice seemed a bit high and thin. *He's scared*, Sheila thought with a surge of excitement.

"They are merely another part of the spectacle," said the emperor. "For tonight not only the unicorns will die, but also"—Dynasian pointed dramatically to the cage that held Laric, a huge noble eagle with a wounded wing—"an enemy of the people, an evil wizard who has brought blight and plague to the land as he flies with his servants disguised as an innocent bird."

A horrified gasp shot through the crowd. The crowd was confused now, Sheila had no doubt. Dynasian's words made her cringe. Her knuckles were white with rage as she clenched the bow under her tunic.

I could kill him now, thought Sheila as she glared at the pig-faced emperor. She shot a glance at Kara, who, as best archer of the group, would take the first shot. That shot was important. Once the arrow left her bow, the battle would begin—there would be no turning back. Sheila gulped back fear. It was all about to happen. . . .

Dynasian seemed near panic. "Let the killing begin!" he shrieked, his voice full of hate and madness.

The executioner stepped to Laric's cage. He drew back his arm, his spear tip trained on Laric's heart. The eagle prince gazed past him, his eyes steady with unbent pride.

At the same instant the spear was about to meet its mark, an arrow whistled through the air.

"Aaaah!" came the strangled cry as the barb plunged deep into the executioner's shoulder.

Kara had fired.

11

❧✦❧

The Great Battle

The executioner staggered back and collapsed in a pool of his own blood. For a few moments no one moved. Not the soldiers. Not Dynasian. Not the hordes of spectators. Not even the unicorn warriors.

Then a single cry broke the silence. Someone in the crowd was cheering. "Freedom!" a woman had shouted. Then someone else took up the cheer. The chant swept like wildfire from the exhausted, oppressed people.

"Freedom!" they cried. They had had enough of Dynasian's tyrannical rule. Kara's single arrow broke the dam of fear that had long held back their outrage. Now the anger caused by many years of suffering and unfairness poured forth from the crowd in a torrent of vengeful cries.

"Freedom!" The shout shook the very foundations of the city. "Freedom!"

Sheila felt the joyous cry resounding within her. Freedom! Maybe now they could achieve it . . . now that the people were with them.

At that moment Darian appeared in the square

with the herd of unicorns. He looked confused. He had been planning to pass the unicorns off as gifts; now there was no need. The fight was on, and the unicorns ran through the crowd, each heading for its rider.

Sheila pulled herself up on Morning Star's back. The unicorn whinnied a jubilant greeting. Sheila knew the unicorn would fight as fiercely as she always had. Feeling the surge of power that always came to her when she rode Morning Star, Sheila felt a new confidence well up inside herself.

"Freed unicorns! Freed people!" someone screamed at the sight of the unicorns.

"Open the pen! Open the pen!" the people cried together as one.

"Silence them!" Dynasian screeched at his soldiers. "Silence them now!"

In horror Sheila watched as the guards turned to obey their leader. The soldiers raised swords and bows and were preparing to shoot right into the crowd. Sheila looked around quickly for her friends. They couldn't let the soldiers do this. It would be a massacre!

Eeeeeee! Seven arrows sailed through the air. Seven guards fell.

Cawwww! Ceeaaawww! Laric's eagles swooped to attack, and more of Dynasian's men tumbled to the ground. The furious birds attacked relentlessly as Illyria's band filled the air with arrows.

Dynasian's soldiers were confused and disorganized at first, but all too soon their spears sailed up toward the eagles. Other guards took on the unicorn warriors. The unicorns reared up and beat back the soldiers with their powerful hoofs. Their horns were sharp and fearsome weapons.

Sheila saw Dynasian struggling down the steps of the platform. She raised her arrow and took aim, but Dynasian spotted her and dropped to his knees and scuttled quickly under the platform, crawling like a scared dog.

Suddenly a bolt of lightning flashed in Sheila's direction. Mardock! Had he seen her, or was this just a random shot? She looked and saw the wizard surrounded by crackling green energy that warded off every arrow that flew in his direction. Sheila saw one of Kara's arrows streak directly toward his heart, but bounce off the energy field.

The battle raged fiercely. Many of the people took up the fight, attacking guards with whatever weapons they could find. The merchant who had walked into the city near her earlier whacked a guard in the face with his heavy pouch of coins. Women smashed soldiers over the head with heavy copper pots and vases they had brought as forced tribute to the emperor.

The less brave members of the crowd surged toward the exits to avoid the flying spears of Dynasian's soldiers. A few of the flaming torches that had been lighting the spectacle went over, and the platform began to burn. As the flames leapt higher, they threw giant shadows and lit the square in a gruesome flickering light.

Still, more people were fighting than panicking.

One wiry little woman was throwing a whole month's tomato crop at the attacking soldiers. The fruit oozed in an ever-reddening mess. Sheila almost wanted to laugh, watching how the old woman was besting the guards. But suddenly the woman screamed, utterly terrified. One huge guard had snuck up behind her. He held her by her hair and raised a knife to her throat. Sheila reached for the bow that she had yet to use in the bloody battle. Without thinking she took aim and let the arrow fly. As it hit its mark, Sheila felt woozy. The guard slumped to the ground, his knife slipping away from the old woman, who turned to see who had saved her. There was too much confusion; the woman waved vaguely, as if to say, thank you, whoever you are. Sheila stared as the woman stepped over the body of the guard and resumed throwing tomatoes.

It was too much to think about just now, Sheila knew. But over and over she saw the arrow hit, the guard slump, the woman smile and wave. Shaking herself roughly, Sheila tried to clear her head. She grasped her bow. Determined not to fall apart, she began firing to knock weapons out of the guards' hands. Her hands were shaking and her first shot missed, almost hitting an innocent woman in the crowd.

Get control of yourself, she thought. She took a deep breath and placed a second arrow in her bow. This time her shot grazed a guard's wrist, and his spear fell to the ground.

"Good shooting!" Kara shouted encouragingly.

Sheila turned toward her friend. "Kara, you're hurt!" She gasped at the sight of the warrior's blood-smeared face. Kara's forehead was opened in a red gash. Her usually ruddy complexion was pale.

"A spear grazed me!" Kara shouted back. "It's just a flesh wound, not important, keep shooting."

Obediently Sheila fired another arrow at a guard, but her hands shook. She needed at least an encouraging look from Kara, but when she turned back, she saw that the archer's expression was stern and concentrated. Her bow was raised.

Sheila followed the direction of Kara's aim as the arrow sliced through the air. Kara was firing right into the pen of captive unicorns!

"What are you doing?" Sheila shouted, a nauseous fear invading every muscle in her body. Had Kara gone totally mad? Had her head wound confused her so that she was trying to shoot the unicorns?

But when the arrow hit its mark, Sheila felt a surge of relief. Kara had shot at the lock that held the pen. The lock cracked, but held firm.

Thwifp! Kara sent another arrow into the night.

"Bull's-eye!" Sheila cried as the lock shuddered and broke in two. The door swung open, and though the unicorns were wild with terror, they hated their captivity and immediately flooded through the narrow entrance. They stampeded out of the pen, leaping off the platform to the ground below.

Some unicorns fell in the rush to escape, but quickly righted themselves on their nimble legs. Even though the unicorns were naturally agile, they were spooked by the battle and the flames licking up on all sides of them. They bucked frantically, neighing with fear.

"You heard your emperor!" Mardock shrieked at the soldiers from the platform where he stood, green energy making him impervious to all danger. "Kill those unicorns!"

Two soldiers tried to obey, aiming their spears into the unicorns, but as they did, they were attacked from behind by the transformed eagle warriors Cam and Gebart, who cut them down quickly with flashing swords.

Many of the unicorns had broken loose and were galloping aimlessly through the embattled crowd. Others were clustered together near the platform area, confused and trapped by a flaming wooden beam that had fallen into their path. With a flourish of his hand, Mardock caused the fire to spread in a circle around the unicorns.

Sheila knew the unicorns might be burned alive, but she didn't know what to do. In the next instant she saw Illyria and Quiet Storm leap higher than ever before, right above the flaming circle and into the midst of the bucking unicorns.

Illyria shouted something to Quiet Storm and then jumped from his back. As Sheila watched, Quiet Storm reared and whinnied an urgent command to the other unicorns. They seemed to gather new resolve, and one by one they leapt fearlessly over the yellow flames.

While Quiet Storm led the unicorns, Illyria let one of the leaping animals carry her back over the fire. She quickly jumped off its back and made her way up to the flaming platform, her sword held high before her.

She faced off with Mardock, slashing her sword at

the green energy field. Sheila saw that Illyria's sword seemed to bounce off the green light as Mardock looked at the Unicorn Queen smugly from within his magical field.

Sheila's heart leapt into her throat when she saw Mardock raise his hands, as if to aim some of his evil magic straight at Illyria.

"Come on, girl!" Sheila shouted to Morning Star. She headed toward the platform with no clear thought in her head except to somehow keep Illyria safe from Mardock's evil.

Morning Star needed no urging, but she was caught in a throng of battling soldiers and citizens. "Look out, Illyria!" Sheila shrieked as Morning Star reared up to avoid the clash of swords below her feet.

Illyria looked at Sheila for a split second and then instantly back to Mardock just in time to see a bolt of green sparkling light heading straight for her. In a blur of speed Illyria held up the blunt end of her sword in front of her.

The gleaming blade crackled like a lightning rod with the energy of Mardock's blast. Just before the jolt of power reached the hilt, Illyria whirled the sword powerfully over her head and threw the bolt of sizzling lightning back at Mardock with all her strength.

Zwap! Mardock's protective field exploded with a burst of bright light. Illyria pounced on the evil wizard like a lioness, but somehow he managed to squirm out of his long black robe and leap off the platform into the crowd. Sheila saw Illyria leap off the platform in hot pursuit.

In the meantime Sheila had worked her way out of the crowd around her and was looking to see where she was most needed by her companions.

She spotted frail Lianne looking bewildered as she stood in the middle of the square holding her bow at her side. Sheila saw a soldier aiming his spear in Lianne's direction. "Behind you, Lianne!" Sheila screamed, but it was clear Lianne hadn't heard her over the roar of battle. Sheila galloped in her direction, and just as the soldier was about to let his spear fly into Lianne's back, Sheila wounded him in the leg with an arrow that whirred from her bow.

Lianne spun around to face Sheila and went pale. In a flash she raised her bow and fired in Sheila's direction. Sheila froze with fright as the arrow whirred past her left shoulder.

Thwump! Sheila pulled Morning Star around and saw one of Dynasian's soldiers fall from a balcony directly behind her. Instantly she knew he had been aiming his spear directly at her.

Her hands trembling from the close call, Sheila waved to Lianne. The dark-haired girl returned the wave with a smile of pride.

The wild unicorns had rallied around Quiet Storm and were attacking Dynasian's army, beating them back without mercy. Sheila had seen unicorns in combat before. They were fierce and inexhaustible, and their flying hoofs and sharp horns never missed their marks.

To the left of Sheila, Nanine and Pelu fought side by side on foot, each of them taking on two guards at once in a clanking battle of swords.

Nanine had worn her golden powder even into battle. Now it ran down her sweat-covered face in golden rivulets that made her look like a tigress.

Pelu's always-neat hair had come completely undone and hung around her shoulders in wheat-colored waves, sticking to her wet forehead. Her thin, well-muscled arms bore down on her opponent, sending his sword flying out of his hands. Sheila knew the gentle woman could hold her own, but she had never seen her fight this relentlessly before.

To her right, Myno, astride her unicorn, routed a group of soldiers with a bullwhip she had yanked away from the soldiers themselves. "Ya, hah!" Sheila heard the burly woman cry. "Run for it, you mangy dogs."

And now Dynasian's guards were boxed in. Illyria's warriors and the freedom-hungry citizens held one front while the unicorns held another. The eagle fighters continued the assault, some as eagles, swooping down on the enemy from above, and others as men on the ground.

Sheila sized up the situation and quickly realized that the emperor's forces were going down! A rousing battle cheer swept through the mass of fearless fighters—man, woman, eagle, and unicorn.

Sheila raised her bow yet again, aiming to shoot. She realized that it was becoming harder and harder to tell friend from foe, even in the firelight of the burning platform. The night seemed to be growing darker.

Looking up, she saw the full, round circle of the moon disappearing. "The eclipse!" she shouted hoarsely. In all the turmoil she had completely forgotten about it and all it meant to Laric and his men.

The eclipse had come and there was no potion for the eagle warriors to drink. There just hadn't been time to do it all. The eagles had decided it was more important to rescue Laric than to spare even one warrior to search for zanga nuts for the magical brew.

They had decided to gamble on the hope that they could seize Mardock before the eclipse and force him to give them the potion. They hadn't counted on what a tough and slippery opponent Mardock really was. Now they would be eagles for who knew how much longer . . . maybe forever.

It can't be, Sheila thought desperately. *There must be a way.* Suddenly Sheila noticed that something strange was going on at one end of the square. She squinted in the darkening night and saw that the fighting had stopped there and everyone—even Dynasian's soldiers—was fleeing the area, shrieking in horrified terror.

What now? Sheila wondered. In the next second she discovered what it was the crowd was trying so frantically to escape. Easing its way through the parting crowd was a sky-blue Ferrari convertible. Behind the wheel sat Dr. Reit, his longish white hair blown into a mess by his trip through the Molecular Acceleration Transport Device.

"Dr. Reit!" Sheila cried. What a time for her old friend to show up! "I'm over here!" she called over the deafening sounds of the battle and the fleeing crowd.

Kara rode up alongside her. "What sort of beast is your friend riding?" she asked, amazed.

"It's not an animal, it's a *car*, a machine," Sheila tried to explain.

Kara's dark eyes widened. "He divined the perfect moment to show up once again. Look, his magic is working already."

Kara was right. Something amazing was happening. The battle was coming to a total halt. Dynasian's soldiers were throwing down their weapons and running for their lives at the sight of this strange machine. Further away, the storm still brewed, but Dr. Reit realized the impact he was having and was delighting in driving all around the square and sending everyone running for safety everywhere he went.

Sheila waved and shouted to her friend, but from the way he almost stood behind the wheel craning his long neck in all directions, she knew he was still looking for her. His kindly dark eyes peered into the crowd, seeking her out.

Not waiting another moment, Sheila forced her way through the throng of people and galloped up to the car. "Dr. Reit, here I am!" she cried.

"So I see, my dear girl," said Dr. Reit happily. "You do manage to get yourself in and out of some interesting situations, don't you." He laughed. "Like the car? I'm sure my brother-in-law won't let me hear the end of it if I get any spear scratches on his new pin-striping."

He let the car idle as he reached into the backseat and picked up a brown cardboard carton filled with small plastic canteens. "I see it's quite dark here, and from that I take it we are now actually in the eclipse you spoke about the other night. Therefore, we will chat later. Right now we must busy ourselves dispersing this potion."

"You made the potion!" Sheila cried.

"I'm not sure of it," he explained hurriedly. "I did my best to find a substitute for the zanga nuts. What I came up with was—"

Dr. Reit interrupted himself, and from the expression on his face, Sheila knew someone was behind her. Sheila whirled around, and there was Mardock.

12
❈ ❖ ❈
The Final Test

The moon was almost completely blotted out, and an uncanny darkness filled the city square. But the evil wizard was clearly visible by the light that came from the flaming platform behind him. Sheila felt the full weight of her fear as he loomed over her.

And then he began to laugh, a laugh so full of malice and violence, Sheila wanted to cover her ears and run.

"Well, my little wizard," Mardock spat out the words with distaste, "it seems I will have the pleasure of dealing with you at last . . . and with your teacher as well." Mardock looked past Sheila to Dr. Reit.

"Leave him alone," Sheila said, summoning her courage. But it was too late. Mardock did not hesitate to blast him with a bolt of green fury, as the scientist stood up in the front seat.

Dr. Reit sat back in the car. In a moment he recovered himself. "Now, see here, Mardock," he said bravely, rising again to confront the evil wizard. "Sheila here is a sweet girl and certainly no one for you to be tormenting in such a rude fashion."

Enraged by Dr. Reit's assertiveness, Mardock sent another green blast surging from his fingertips.

Dr. Reit was hit in the chest with a blast so powerful it flipped him over the windshield and onto the hood of the convertible.

"Dr. Reit!" Sheila screamed.

The scientist struggled to his feet, waving one hand as if to say he was all right—or at least alive. But he was weak, and the blast had knocked the wind out of him.

"So much for your wizard!" Mardock laughed. "I did not kill him because he may prove useful. He may teach me some science magic. But you . . ." Mardock stepped closer to Sheila. "You I have no use for."

Morning Star reared up at Mardock, but the wizard seemed unafraid. Fearing that Mardock would zap her unicorn as well, Sheila quieted the angry animal.

Sheila glanced back at Dr. Reit and saw him edging his way toward the front seat of the car from where he lay on the hood. She had to give him credit for being tough, but his face looked worn from Mardock's attacks. If he could get back into the car, maybe he could gun the motor and at least save himself from being Mardock's servant.

Dr. Reit had slipped from the hood and crept into the car by way of the passenger entrance. Apparently, he had thought of the same plan as Sheila had and was hoping not to attract Mardock's attention.

It wasn't working, though. Mardock focused his steely glare on the old scientist once again.

"Dr. Reit, go!" Sheila yelled when she saw that he was in the car.

"Silence!" demanded Mardock, a spasm of green flashing out at her. "You have upset my plans for the last time, child. I may not get the unicorn powder tonight, but Laric and his men will be trapped forever in my enchantment. And I will have my revenge on you!" As he readied himself to cast some terrible spell on Sheila, she saw that Darian and Illyria had quietly moved through the crowd and were now standing close behind him, near the flaming platform.

They were going to save her! Sheila felt one moment of hope, then realized she had been wrong. Illyria and Darian were taking this opportunity to rescue Laric. The platform was burning out of control, and Laric's cage was close to the flames. Sheila knew that Illyria would expect her to fight Mardock with "sorcery" of her own. But Sheila didn't have any magic . . . or did she? At the same moment that Mardock raised his hands and began an incantation that made her insides twist into knots, Sheila cried, "Headlights! Dr. Reit, hit the headlights!"

In the next instant the scene was flooded with bright white light.

"Aaaagg," Mardock cringed, covering his eyes and cursing. Sheila knew it would take only a moment for him to recover. Soon enough he would realize the light would not injure him.

There was another flash of light, or rather a brighter one. Dr. Reit was flashing the Ferrari's high beams.

"Enough!" Mardock raged. He spun at the blinding beams and shot green fire into them. With a shattering of glass, the lights went out. As a last resort Dr. Reit leaned on the car horn.

"Stop playing with your toys, you're making me angry!" Mardock screamed.

Mardock flung another blast of energy at Dr. Reit, throwing him back against the front seat of the car. Then Mardock pointed one long finger at Sheila. "You are out of time, my little sorceress," he snarled.

Sheila shuddered. She had no more tricks. This was the end of the line for her.

"Caaaawwww!" A gold streak shot down from above. It was Laric. Darian and Illyria had set him free. Laric dived toward the sorcerer, his talons outstretched. His dark nails tore at Mardock's black silk cape.

"Stop this, you foul bird!" Mardock cried, cowering.

As the sorcerer stumbled out of the eagle's reach, he was attacked again. The Unicorn Queen caught him off guard. She brought the flat side of her blade down hard against the back of his neck. Sheila had never seen Illyria fight with such passion. Her strength was astonishing. Under normal circumstances she would never have gotten close enough to Mardock to hit him. Now that she had him staggering, unable to recover long enough to fight her off with magic, she was unrelenting. Finally Mardock collapsed under Illyria's blows. Illyria raised her sword as if to plunge it into the evil wizard.

"No!" shouted Laric, now transformed to his human form. "Mardock is a mage. You cannot kill him that way. Leave him to me."

Illyria stepped back and lowered her sword. In the flickering light of the flames Sheila saw that the Unicorn Queen's face was wet with tears. Her eyes glittered. She looked at Laric for a long moment. "It is too late," she said, looking up at the moon. The eclipse had almost ended.

13
❧❧❧
Freedom!

Dr. Reit stirred in the front seat of the car. "That . . . that beam," he muttered. "If I could figure out what it's composed of, I'd revolutionize science."

"Dr. Reit!" Sheila cried. "Quickly—give us the potion you brought."

"Yes, indeed." Dr. Reit took six canteens out and handed the carton with the other six up to Sheila. "I'll hand these out, and you give out the rest. Maybe we can make it."

Laric was struggling with Mardock, so Sheila passed the first canteen to Illyria, who quickly pulled the top off and put it to Laric's lips. Then Sheila set off at a gallop, throwing her six canteens of potion to the battling eagle warriors, who had transformed into their human form. "Drink quickly!" she shouted. She saw Dr. Reit driving around in the convertible doing the same.

The eagle warriors were busy fighting the last of Laric's men. When they saw their chance for freedom, they made short work of their enemies and guzzled the sweet liquid.

The last to receive the potion was Cam. Sheila stopped Morning Star beside him and watched him hopefully. Cam threw the canteen down and closed his eyes. He seemed to tense every muscle in his strong body. He clenched his fists in front of his face and waited . . . waited for feathers to sprout and a beak to form where his nose and mouth had been. He waited to grow talons on his feet and for strong wings to appear where his arms once were.

Sheila waited, too. She watched for the first signs of the golden glow that indicated the magic transformation from man to eagle was beginning. She studied Cam, not taking her eyes from him and barely breathing. The potion had to work . . . it just had to.

Slowly Cam opened his eyes. Finger by finger he unclenched the fists in front of his face. He stared at his broad hands as if he had never seen them before, and then a wide smile broke across his weathered face. "I can't change into an eagle!" he shouted. "It worked! By the gods, it worked!"

As he spoke, Sheila noticed a line of silver moonlight running down the side of his face. "Just in time," she said with a sigh of relief. The lunar eclipse was over.

Sheila felt tears of happiness rushing to her eyes. They had done it! They had really done it! It had seemed impossible, but now Sheila was aware of the shouts of Laric's men as one by one they realized the potion had worked.

She saw Gebart and Atmar hugging each other and laughing. The other warriors, too, sent up cheers from every corner of the square. All twelve of them were shouting and leaping with happiness.

Two of the warriors sat in the front of Dr. Reit's convertible and honked gleefully on his horn. Sheila caught the scientist's eyes and smiled. He smiled back, his dark eyes crinkling happily.

In the spreading light Sheila could see that they had won the battle. Dynasian's soldiers were either down or had fled.

She suddenly realized that she hadn't seen Laric since she handed Illyria the canteen of potion. She turned Morning Star around and galloped back to the place where she'd left them.

"How's Laric? Did it work?" she shouted when she caught sight of Illyria. The Unicorn Queen turned quickly and held up her hand to silence Sheila. With a quick smile she said, "Laric is fine. The potion worked, but now he can't be disturbed."

Sheila saw that Laric was standing over the prone Mardock with his arms outstretched. Nanine and Myno assisted Laric by sitting on Mardock's shoulders and chest. Lianne held down his ankles, while Laric recited strange words over him.

"By the alpha sun and the omega star, shed this form and be what you are," she heard Laric's rich voice finish the magic incantation.

On the ground Mardock screamed as if some terrible acid were eating him alive. His body shuddered violently, and the women had to press with all their might to keep him pinned. He kicked wildly, sending Lianne sprawling, but she quickly scrambled back, aided this time by Darian, who pressed his weight on Mardock's other leg.

"I curse you for this by the power of Medusa . . ." Mardock began, uttering one last desperate spell. Realizing what he was up to, Sheila slid off Morning Star's back, reached into her backpack, and pulled out her extra pair of gym socks. As quickly as possible she stuffed them into Mardock's mouth, keeping him from finishing his spell.

Mardock's eyes blazed at her in a fury so frightening that Sheila stepped back away from him.

"The bag of science does it again!" Darian said proudly as he pressed down on the still-struggling Mardock. "I told you there was still more magic in that bag."

"I wouldn't call it magic, or sciences," said Sheila, laughing, "but it did the trick, all right."

Suddenly a great, green flash sent Sheila and the others staggering backward. The rotten egg smell of burning sulphur accompanied the light, which grew brighter and brighter.

The warriors gagged and shielded their eyes. When Sheila looked again, a giant water bug was all that remained in the spot where Mardock had been. It fluttered its horrid blackish wings and flew away, disappearing into the night.

"Mardock has been destroyed!" someone in the crowd shouted.

"We are free of his evil magic forever!" a woman shouted.

The square was once again lit by the brightness of the full moon. All around Sheila people were cheering and hugging one another jubilantly. They were sweaty and bloodstained, but they wore expressions of total joy. They had helped to win their own freedom.

The citizens weren't the only ones celebrating. The herd of freed unicorns mixed with those of Illyria's riders and galloped happily around the square. In the center of them Quiet Storm reared up with pleasure. "I guess you'd like to join them, Star," Sheila said. She hugged her unicorn, who whinnied happily in response and then, with a pat on the side from Sheila, went to join the other unicorns.

Sheila waved to Dr. Reit, who was driving toward her in the convertible. He waved back looking exhilarated despite being zapped by Mardock's blasts. His agile mind craved new experience, and this was the experience of a lifetime.

"Dr. Reit," Sheila asked when he pulled up alongside her, "where did you ever find zanga nuts?"

"As I was saying," said Dr. Reit happily, "I took an educated guess and hoped that zanga nuts would be equivalent to our cola nuts. Frankly, with that substitution it is basically just a cola drink formula. It was the only substitution that fit. Still, it was a longshot."

Sheila threw her arms around Dr. Reit. "You're a genius! A true genius!" she cried.

"Yes, well, so I've been told," Dr. Reit muttered happily. "Still, it's nice to hear it."

Sheila looked over at her friends, who were standing together several feet away. Everyone but Illyria was rejoicing. Her expression was serious, and her blue eyes were scanning the square intently, as if seeking something she had lost. What could be wrong? "I'll be right back," she told Dr. Reit.

"What's the matter?" Sheila asked, racing up to the pensive Illyria.

"We are not done yet," Illyria said quietly. "Come."

Illyria took Sheila's arm and led her to the center of the warriors. "My friends!" she shouted. "We have left a deadly loose end hanging, and we must tie it up forever before our work here is done."

"Dynasian," said Laric, as if reading her mind.

"Dynasian," Sheila echoed glumly.

"Think!" Illyria commanded the group. "Where did you last see him?"

Sheila closed her eyes, concentrating hard. She *had* seen the emperor; she remembered how she had ached to pull out her bow and shoot him.

Dynasian had been on the platform when he had ordered the executioner to kill Laric. Then Kara's arrow had stopped the executioner. Dynasian had turned the soldiers loose on the crowd and . . . and then everything had gone crazy.

But an image was floating somewhere in the back of Sheila's mind. She saw him again, dropping to his knees and crawling underneath the platform.

Sheila's eyes snapped open. "I remember," she said. "He hid under the platform. I saw him."

"That platform is almost burned to the ground," said Dian, who, along with Pelu, had now joined the others.

"He couldn't still be hiding under there," added Darian.

"I guess that doesn't really help much then," said Sheila.

"On the contrary," Illyria said, striding toward the center of the spot where the platform once stood. "You have told me all I need to know." Sheila didn't understand.

"But, Illyria, he couldn't still be there." Sheila ran to join the Unicorn Queen. They picked their way carefully through the embers and smoldering timbers. Smoke rose from the ashes, and the ground felt hot under Sheila's feet.

"Ah, but he is," said Illyria mysteriously. "You do not understand much of the ways of kings, Sheila." Illyria pointed to a spot a few feet from them. Beneath a pile of smoking curtains and beams, a glimmer of gold shone in the moonlight.

Sheila gasped. "But how?"

"I would have been surprised if the emperor had *not* had some place to secrete himself, or the treasures he planned to steal from the people. There is a trap door. He thinks he is safely hidden, but his pride and excess have given him away. That," Illyria said with a smile, "is the hem of his robe. Had he worn a simpler garment, he might have escaped our notice."

With relish, Illyria stomped unheedful of the heat and smoke to the spot where the trap door was. Grabbing a beam that had not been too badly burned, she shoved away the pile that covered the door. A small iron handle was fit snugly into the stone pavement. The Unicorn Queen grasped it and flung the door open.

"Come out, vermin!" Illyria commanded.

Slowly and with some difficulty, Dynasian slithered up out of his hiding place. He hugged a sack of gold to his chest and pulled his gleaming robe around him. On his head a sparkling golden circlet listed to one side.

The emperor's eyes darted from side to side. Sheila could see the terror rising in him. Laric's men and the warrior women had moved to stand in a wide circle around the spot where the platform had burned. Behind them the unicorns paced, restless and hostile.

As she surveyed the scene, Sheila saw that Dr. Reit was trying to get her attention. He was waving frantically. When he caught her eye, he called out. "Sheila, we've got to—" But he was interrupted.

In his desperation Dynasian had lunged for Illyria. The Unicorn Queen fought him off but noticed the glint of a knife in his hand a moment too late. Illyria cried out as the blade slashed her cheek.

"No!" Sheila cried. Not knowing what else to do, she ran headlong toward the crazed emperor.

Dynasian shrieked as Sheila knocked him away from Illyria. She fell to the ground on top of him, but Dynasian leapt up like a desperate wild animal. He still had his dagger. "You'll never take me!" he cried. "I am the emperor of Campora! Nothing can change that!"

Dynasian waved his dagger at Sheila. In seconds Myno and Nanine held his two arms behind him. He seemed to have lost his senses and raged like a madman.

"No more," Illyria said, resting her sword's tip lightly on the emperor's chin. "You've hurt enough people. You've made too many pay for your greediness. Now *you* will pay for their suffering."

Dynasian seemed to see Illyria for the first time. "You," he said. "You are the one they call the Unicorn Queen. It's you who have done this to me, you and your wretched warriors. I will not be bested by a group of ragtag women!"

"You have done this to yourself, Dynasian," Illyria answered harshly. Her braids had come loose and her silver-blond hair hung around her shoulders like a wild halo, making her seem to radiate energy and power.

She stepped in even closer to Dynasian. "You killed my family, stole the unicorns who belong only to those they choose. Your wizard bespelled the rightful ruler of this land, and you have tormented and enslaved your people. Why should I spare your worthless little life?"

For a moment Sheila thought Illyria would run her sword through Dynasian and kill him on the spot.

"I would be happy to kill you now," said the warrior-woman. "But that is not the right way. You will be judged and punished by the people you have so foully mistreated." She brought her sword to her side and slipped it into its sheath. "He must be taken to the dungeons," Illyria said to the warriors who stood around her. Laric stepped toward her.

"My men will take him and guard him well," he said. Cam and Darian dragged Dynasian up, bound his wrists, and began marching him through the square. They had gone only a few feet when Dr. Reit gunned the engine of the Ferrari.

"Sheila!" he cried desperately. Again he was trying to get her attention, and again events tore her away.

The sudden noise of the engine had startled Cam and Darian, and they had loosened their grip on Dynasian—only for an instant. But an instant was all he needed. The insane emperor began to run away. His attempt was futile, but he seemed beyond that understanding. Laric's men hurried to catch him and would have if something had not prevented them.

It was Quiet Storm. The unicorn seemed to appear from nowhere as the emperor made a mad dash toward an alleyway.

"No!" Illyria shouted. "You must not!" She feared Quiet Storm would impale Dynasian to make him pay for all his crimes. And it seemed that was Quiet Storm's intention.

Quiet Storm had Dynasian cornered. He looked at Illyria, and there was no doubt he heard her words. Nonetheless, he turned toward Dynasian, his eyes flashing angrily at the captive dictator.

The powerful white unicorn advanced, and Dynasian stepped backward, a trapped look on his fat face. There was no escape for him. Quiet Storm was only inches away. But the unicorn didn't charge the sniveling man.

Instead, inexplicably, Quiet Storm lowered his horn and caught the hem of Dynasian's golden robe. At the instant the unicorn's horn touched the cloth there was a tremendous flash of sick green light.

The astonished warriors gaped at the spot where Dynasian had been. The dreaded ruler had disintegrated, leaving only a few flecks of ashen powder on the ground.

For a moment there was silence among the warriors—shocked, uncomprehending silence.

"Wh—what?" Sheila sputtered.

Laric stepped forward, leaning down to inspect Dynasian's dusty remains. "Magic," he pronounced, straightening up. "Sorcery of the darkest kind."

Sheila looked at the gray dust, and a thought came to her. That robe was made of the material from Mardock's chamber. Somehow it was the key to Dynasian's end.

"I have an idea," she said to the others, the whole strange series of events taking shape in her mind as she spoke. "Mardock did it. The cloth was enchanted. He must have planned to destroy the emperor once the unicorn horn had been ground up. He wanted the unicorn powder, the wealth, and the empire—everything—for himself. Dynasian would have been turned to ashes tonight no matter what he did because of the spell Mardock put on that material."

"And Mardock would have stepped in," said Laric. "Tonight we've saved the land from a fate even worse than Dynasian's cruelty."

"And restored its good and noble ruler," added Illyria, coming up behind Laric and putting her arms gently around his shoulders. Her face was soft with tenderness when she looked at him. "If Dynasian's executioner had done his work . . ." Illyria was unable to finish her words; she simply smoothed Laric's forehead lovingly with her hands.

14
❧❖❧
Changes

Laric turned to face his beloved Illyria. "The danger is over, and we have won," he said warmly, wiping a trickle of blood gently from the thin wound Dynasian had made in her beautiful high cheek.

"Now I can be the husband you deserve. The Unicorn Queen will soon be the queen of all the land . . ." Laric hesitated a moment and searched Illyria's clear blue eyes. "If that is your wish," he added, almost shyly.

Illyria's face broke into a radiant smile. "Gladly would I spend my life with you, Laric, be it as queen or commoner," she said.

"And I thought she didn't care," Lianne whispered to Sheila.

"I never saw anyone care so much in my life," Sheila replied with a smile.

More sounds of jubilation filled the square. People everywhere had linked arms and were singing songs of freedom. The unicorn warriors and Laric's men were already swapping battle stories and comparing wounds.

Illyria raised her hands to quiet them. Solemnly

she raised her sword in the air. "To you, brave warriors all. I salute your bravery, your love of the unicorns, and your devotion to all that is good about our people and our land."

"Long live Illyria and Laric!" cried Cam, spinning Myno around in a dance of joy.

"To Illyria and Laric!" cried the women happily, raising their bows in salute.

Dr. Reit had driven over and tooted out a short version of "Here Comes the Bride" on the horn. Everyone looked at him quizzically. "Just a tradition of a nuptial celebration from back home," he explained happily, tooting out the tune again.

At the mention of home Dr. Reit looked down at the dashboard. "Good gracious," he muttered. "Sheila, I hate to rush you at a time like this, but I'm almost on empty. If we run out of gas and this engine dies, then I'm afraid we'll be stuck here forever, and . . . well, as delightful and enchanting as these people are . . ."

Suddenly the reality of the situation came tumbling in on Sheila. She couldn't go home now! Not now, when the danger and fighting were finally over and when everything had worked out so well.

Sheila bit her lip. Life in this land was going to improve drastically in the coming days. There would be work, but it would be the work of rebuilding and making beautiful again the life that Dynasian and Mardock had tried to destroy. She wanted to be a part of it.

"Sheila, I'm afraid you must decide rather quickly," Dr. Reit urged her.

Sheila had to think fast. Could she really give it all up? She looked around at her friends. They looked back at her, awaiting her decision.

Morning Star sensed her dilemma and broke free of the other unicorns. She cantered over and nuzzled Sheila gently on the arm. Sheila hugged the unicorn around the neck. Her eyes brimmed with tears at the thought of leaving her trusted friend. There were no unicorns at home, and even if there were, Sheila was sure there would never be one she would love like this creamy filly.

Darian walked up beside her. His deep brown eyes seemed to be asking her not to go. He was the first boy she had ever kissed—the first boy she ever felt so strongly about. She wondered if she would be able to feel that way about anyone else. He reached out and held her hand.

She took it and squeezed it hard. She looked around at her friends: Myno. Nanine. Pelu. Kara. Lianne. Laric's warriors. Would she ever enjoy the camaraderie of such brave and loyal friends again?

But then other pictures came into her mind. Her mother and father. Her best friend, Cookie. Her dream of going to college and studying to someday be an astronaut. She didn't want to give up these people and the future she had planned for herself.

"I have to go," she whispered gently to Darian. "I'll never forget you. Never."

Darian turned away and wiped his eyes quickly with the palms of his hands. "I know, Sheila," he said in a voice choked with emotion. "I'll never forget you, either." He grabbed her tightly and held her to him. She wet his rough tunic with the water from her tears.

"Sheila, I'm idling on fumes, I'm sorry," Dr. Reit said, imploring her to hurry.

Darian looked at her and nodded as if to say he understood her decision. She squeezed him one more time and turned toward the others.

Illyria approached and embraced her. "Go home knowing that you are one of the bravest warriors I have ever met, Sheila from the Land of Science. My love and thanks follow you through time and space." Illyria pulled one of her silver bracelets from her arm and slipped it onto Sheila's arm. "Take this as small thanks from one to whom you have given much."

Sheila hugged Illyria. "No one has ever taught me more than you," she said, tears now running freely down her face.

"You saved my life today," Illyria told her with a smile. "When Mardock threw his evil green lightning my way this day, I saw you calling to me and recalled how you had once used your mirror to throw Mardock's spell back upon him. I did the same with my sword."

Sheila smiled and wiped her eyes. Illyria's words filled her with happy pride.

"Hurry now, Sheila," Illyria said in the voice of gentle command Sheila had heard so many times before. "Our dear Dr. Reit is growing anxious."

Quickly Sheila hugged each of the women.

"I told you the magic inside you would triumph, little sorceress," Nanine whispered.

"Be well always," said Pelu.

"Your aim is as true as your heart, dear friend," Kara said, throwing her arms around Sheila. Lianne, too, hugged her warmly.

To Sheila's surprise Myno was sobbing so much she could barely speak. She hugged Sheila so hard Sheila heard her own back crack slightly. "I know you will grow up to be a queen among warriors in your own land," she said through her tears. Sheila hugged the gruff, good-hearted woman fiercely.

Laric kissed her quickly on the cheek, and his men bowed to Sheila as one.

Sheila heard the engine of the convertible sputter. She ran toward the car, and as she did, she caught sight of Dian standing off to the side staring at her with a sullen expression, yet with wet eyes. With little time to spare Sheila whipped off the backpack that still hung off her shoulders and tossed it to Dian.

Dian smiled at her and waved. Sheila waved back as she jumped into the convertible beside Dr. Reit. "Here we go," he said.

He stepped on the gas, and the last sight Sheila saw was that of the warriors standing in the square, the fires of the battle still illuminating their proud faces as they raised their weapons high to salute her. In the center, her sword held high in respect, stood Illyria, the Unicorn Queen.

The next thing Sheila knew she was whirling

through an ash-blue void with a cold wind whipping all around her, and then, with a jarring thud, the car landed on its tires in Dr. Reit's backyard.

"We made it," said Dr. Reit, smoothing down his white hair.

Sheila looked around at the familiar surroundings. Dr. Reit's large yard with the wicker lawn furniture. His cat, Einstein, asleep on the back steps, waiting to trip someone up, as usual.

It was all the same. Everything was unchanged—everything but her. In what had been only a few moments in this world, Sheila had lived the adventure of a lifetime.

"It's almost dinnertime, and I believe we'll have to get you freshened up before sending you home," Dr. Reit said.

"Home," she repeated with a mixture of joy and sadness. "Home."

SECRET THE OF THE
Unicorn Queen

The unicorns have been freed, Laric and his men have been returned to their human form, and Sheila has been transported home.

But Sheila's experiences in the land of the Unicorn Queen have changed her from an ordinary teenager to a warrior. Will she be content to just play softball, go to school, and hang out with Cookie? Will Sheila long for her friends and her unicorn? Will she fall through Dr. Reit's molecular transport machine again?

Find out all the answers as the exciting adventure continues in

**THE SECRET OF THE UNICORN QUEEN:
BOOK 4
INTO THE DREAM**